"Going to tell me?"

Nicola chewed her lip. "No."

"So it's something else I don't need to worry about?"

"No. I mean, no, you don't have to worry."

He raised an amused eyebrow. "I'd still rather know."

"Brett, don't be difficult," she protested. "It...wasn't anything much."

"All the more reason not to want to hide it from me," he countered mildly.

She clicked her tongue frustratedly. "You're impossible. All *right*, but don't blame me if you don't like it. I was wondering—just as a natural impulse, what it would be like if we...made love. That's all."

LINDSAY ARMSTRONG was born in South Africa but now lives in Australia with her New Zealand-born husband and their five children. They have lived in nearly every state of Australia and tried their hand at some unusual—for them—occupations, such as farming and horse training, all grist to the mill for a writer! Lindsay started writing romances when their youngest child began school and she was left feeling at a loose end. She is still doing it and loving it.

Books by Lindsay Armstrong

HARLEQUIN PRESENTS®
1946—WHEN ENEMIES MARRY...
1986—ACCIDENTAL NANNY

Don't miss any of our special offers. Write to us at the following address for information on our newest releases.

Harlequin Reader Service
U.S.: 3010 Walden Ave., P.O. Box 1325, Buffalo, NY 14269
Canadian: P.O. Box 609, Fort Erie, Ont. L2A 5X3

LINDSAY ARMSTRONG

He's My Husband!

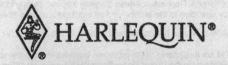

TORONTO • NEW YORK • LONDON
AMSTERDAM • PARIS • SYDNEY • HAMBURG
STOCKHOLM • ATHENS • TOKYO • MILAN • MADRID
PRAGUE • WARSAW • BUDAPEST • AUCKLAND

ISBN 0-373-12040-0

HE'S MY HUSBAND!

First North American Publication 1999.

CHAPTER ONE

THE marriage counsellor was a man in his middle to late thirties.

Nicola Harcourt looked doubtful, and sat down reluctantly. She'd begun to regret this impulse almost as soon as she'd stepped over the doorstep, but now more than ever. A comfortable, middle-aged woman was whom she'd envisaged talking to, a mother figure, perhaps, definitely not a man, and a youngish one at that.

'How may I help you?' the man asked, and smiled ruefully at her obvious wariness. 'I'm the Reverend Peter Callam.' He looked at her enquiringly.

'I think I'll stick to first names, if you don't mind. I'm Nicola.'

'That's fine with me, Nicola. Does it help to know that I'm a minister of religion and I've had specific training in helping troubled marriages?'

'Oh.' Nicola's expression cleared a little. 'Well, yes,' she conceded, then shrugged. 'The thing is, I'm not sure I should be doing this.'

'When one is desperate it's a very good idea to talk things over with a third party who can take an impartial view—'

'I'm not desperate,' Nicola broke in to say.

'Then you're concerned your husband would not appreciate your doing this?'

Nicola grinned. 'I'm sure he wouldn't. But that doesn't really bother me.'

Peter Callam took a moment to study her and to form the impression that this Nicola was unusually attractive. Twenty-one at the most, he guessed, with fair shining hair in a smooth straight fall to below her shoulders, she had deep blue eyes with an exotic fringe of lashes expertly darkened, a straight little nose and a chiselled mouth innocent of any lipstick.

There was also a patina not only of health in her smooth, glowing skin and bright eyes, but wealth in her beautifully cut clothes: a short grey and white checked A-line dress under a charcoal linen jacket with a grey stripe, black leather platform shoes with high chunky heels that emphasised a pair of long golden legs, a black leather tote bag and a pair of designer sunglasses resting on top of her head.

Her only jewellery was a narrow gold wedding band on her left hand.

He frowned slightly and decided to take the direct approach. 'If you're not desperate then why are you here?'

Nicola moved in her chair. 'I am, in a way. The thing is...' She paused, shook her head and sighed. 'I want to leave my husband, who is not the slightest bit in love with me anyway.'

The marriage counsellor clasped his hands on the desk. 'You mean he's fallen out of love with you? He has other women—he abuses you?'

Nicola blinked, an expression of surprise chasing through her deep blue eyes. 'He never lays a finger on me. He's...rather nice—when, that is—' she paused to chew her lip, a rather endearing trait Peter

Callam found himself thinking, despite himself '—he's not being perfectly horrible to me.'

'Ah.' He sat up. 'Mental cruelty can be as bad as the physical kind, and certainly grounds for some kind of intervention.'

Nicola wrinkled her nose. 'It's not that kind of mental cruelty,' she said with a spark of amusement. 'He...we're not really married. I mean, we are, but it was a marriage of convenience, so we live separate lives in the same house kind of thing.' She stopped, then added prosaically, 'We've never slept together.'

'I see. Why did he marry you, then?'

'I'm good with his kids.'

The marriage counsellor gazed at her bemusedly. 'And that's the *only* reason he married you?'

Nicola moved again, uncomfortably this time. 'Oh, well,' she murmured, 'I might as well be hanged for a sheep. This is completely confidential, I presume?' She eyed him with some hauteur.

'Completely.'

'Well, he's also my trustee. He was my father's partner, and when my father died—my mother died when I was two—he took over the reins, so to speak. And when I—er—got myself into a very awkward situation with a man two years ago he said—he *suggested*—a marriage of convenience. I inherited rather a lot of money, you see, which made me the target of—well, I won't go into that, but...' She gestured.

'And now you want out?'

'Would you care to be married for your child-handling abilities and only to keep you out of trouble?' Nicola asked with a lift of an eyebrow.

'Probably not, but it seems to me all you need is

to get yourself a good lawyer and get your marriage annulled on the grounds of it never being consummated.'

Nicola eyed him. 'It's not that simple. For one thing, my husband *is* the best lawyer in town. For another, the provisions of my father's will don't allow me to touch my inheritance until I'm twenty-three. And, because my husband is also my trustee, he's not only my husband but my—jailer, if you see what I mean.'

'He holds the purse strings, in other words?'

'Precisely. You're fairly quick on the uptake, Reverend,' she said, with that glimmer of humour in her eyes again.

And I can't quite imagine the man who wouldn't want a peach of a girl like you, Nicola, the Reverend Peter Callam thought, and flinched inwardly. He said, 'I'm at a bit of a loss, however, Nicola. I generally try to patch marriages up, not break them down, but…are you saying he'd cast you out without a cent if you refused to stay married to him until you're twenty-three?'

'I wouldn't put it past him,' Nicola replied darkly, then grimaced. 'No, of course he wouldn't, but he just won't believe that I can take care of myself. He treats me as if I were one of his kids at times.'

'These children—don't they have a mother?'

'Yes, they do. She was his first wife. They got divorced a few years ago. They had a very turbulent marriage; she's a classical pianist and extremely beautiful—but quite mad, if you want my opinion,' Nicola said candidly. 'And, because she spends a lot of time overseas on concert tours, the children spend a lot more time with their father—which is where I come in.'

'You know their mother well?'

'I've known her all my life. I like her, despite the fact I think she's as mad as a hatter.'

'How many children are there?' Peter Callam asked cautiously, feeling a sudden kinship with Alice in Wonderland.

'Two. A girl of six and a boy of five. They're very naughty and very lovable.' Nicola's lips curved into a warm smile.

'So you wouldn't like to traumatise them—would I be right in assuming that?' he said slowly, but with a keen little glance at Nicola.

She sat forward suddenly. 'What I would really like is to get out of this farce of a marriage as amicably as possible. I'd like to see them all happy—the children, B... my husband, and their mother.'

'The first wife?' Peter Callam blinked. 'But surely—?'

'Surely, yes,' Nicola said, and looked briefly saddened.

Then she went on. 'The thing is, they may not be able to live together, but I'm sure he doesn't want to get seriously involved with anyone else—and that's why I'm so suitable. I run his house, look after his children, I'm his hostess when he needs one, and any...' she paused and shrugged '...physical needs he has are taken care of by a series of sophisticated mistresses whose eyes,' she said with great feeling, 'I'm seriously tempted to scratch out at times!'

'He parades his mistresses in front of you?'

'No, he doesn't,' Nicola said impatiently. 'But I'm

not a fool. I'm sure they must exist. He has an awful lot going for him.'

'All the same, why would you want to scratch the eyes out of these possibly mythical mistresses if you're so determined to leave him?'

The question fell into a pool of silence, and Nicola paled slightly but didn't attempt to drop her blue gaze from his. Then she said huskily, 'The thing is, I fell in love with him—that's why I agreed to this marriage. I thought, in my youth and immaturity—' She grimaced. 'I thought I could make the fairy tale come true and supplant M... his first wife in his heart. But he never did fall in love with me and he never will. Now do you see, Reverend?'

'Yes. I'm sorry, Nicola,' he said compassionately. 'But—'

'No.' She lifted a hand. 'If you're going to offer me platitudes and tell me not to give up hope, don't bother. I'll be twenty-one in two short weeks' time; I've been married to him for two years—I *know* when I'm beaten.'

Nicola stopped and smiled slightly. 'I'm not being very fair to you, am I? But, if it's any help to you, it's been a bit of a help to me to actually say all this— get it off my chest.' She looked wry.

'Thank you,' Peter Callam murmured. 'But I'm still confused. How long *does* he plan to keep you in a marriage of convenience? Because I'm wondering whether he deserves your love, this man, if he's— forgive me—that insensitive apart from anything else, when he knows how you feel, but—'

'Oh, he doesn't know,' Nicola said blithely.

'He doesn't?' Peter Callam blinked.

'You don't think—' She broke off and laughed. 'I may have been young and immature, but I wasn't so immature as to let him see I was madly in love with him.'

'I see.'

'Well, wouldn't you have?'

'Hidden my real feelings?' Peter Callam said slowly. 'I...'

She chuckled after a moment. 'It's an awkward one, isn't it, Reverend? But I can assure you that if you have an ounce of pride, when you're presented with a very definite marriage of convenience, despite all your dreams, you do tend to hide things.'

'I believe you, Nicola. Yet,' he said thoughtfully, 'despite this show of spirited rebellion—' he raised an eyebrow and after a moment she nodded ruefully '—all along you were hoping he'd fall in love with you?'

Her eyes sparkled humorously again. 'I don't fight him all the time. Sometimes we get on like a house on fire.'

'Sounds as if he takes good care of you, then.'

'He does. It's not the kind of care I want taken of me, though.'

'Why *is* that, do you think?'

Nicola considered. 'Not because he's nurturing a secret passion, unfortunately, Reverend,' she said at last. 'It's because of my father. Not only were they partners, but he had great admiration for my father— he wouldn't be where he is today without Daddy's help. I think he looks upon it as a way of repaying a debt to my father.'

'Nicola—' Peter Callam sat forward intently

'—this is the last kind of advice I normally give, believe me, but if you do love this man, if you seriously
think he's worthy of your love, there is a time-
honoured way of getting a man to reveal himself. Not
only to others, but to himself.'

Nicola blinked. 'How?'

'If he thought you were interested in someone else,
that might just...do the trick.' I don't believe I said
that, the Reverend Callam thought, no sooner had he
said it, but this golden girl touched him; he couldn't
deny it.

Nicola wrinkled her brow. 'Make him jealous? That
doesn't sound very Christian, if you don't mind me
saying so, Reverend.'

Peter Callam flinched again, then he had to laugh.
'You're right, but desperate situations require desperate means at times. Not that I would advise you to
actually—'

'Commit adultery?' Nicola suggested with some
irony.

'Most certainly not. Um...does anyone know how
things stand? His first wife, for example?'

'No one really knows, although some people might
suspect. I'm not sure what Marietta thinks. She's usually amazingly, even embarrassingly forthright, but
she just—' Nicola shrugged '—wished me luck and
carried on as if it was a *fait accompli*. I suppose, if
you look at it another way, it's also her children I'm
good with,' she added ruefully.

'But you suspect she may still be in love with him?'

'I think there's a kind of fatal attraction between
them and there always will be.'

'I still feel you shouldn't walk away from this marriage without one last test,' he said stubbornly.

'You probably don't think I can take care of myself either,' Nicola observed.

'I don't think it's a bad thing to be preserved from fortune-hunters until you're twenty-three, Nicola. It's no great age. And you never know.'

Nicola stood up and regarded him quizzically, as if to say, I might have known. What she did say was, 'Look, don't you worry about it, Reverend. I always knew there wasn't going to be an easy solution. Not that that will stop me from trying to find one. But thanks for listening. I feel a bit guilty about taking up your time. I'm sure there are much more worthy causes and desperate women you could really help.'

Peter Callam stood up and handed her a card. 'My time,' he said quietly, 'is always available to those in need, even if it's only to listen.'

Nicola stared at him, then smiled at him radiantly. 'It's people like you, Reverend, who restore one's faith. Thanks a million.' With that, she left.

Brett Harcourt drummed his fingers impatiently on the steering wheel of his sapphire-blue BMW convertible as he waited at a traffic light. The hood was down, although, for Cairns, it was a cooler day than the fierce heat of summer. He was late for an appointment, and every traffic light, this one included, had gone against him at the last minute—and this one took an age to change, he well knew.

Then he frowned as his gaze rested on someone coming out of the Lifeline offices opposite him—his wife. But she didn't cross the road in front of him,

although for her the light was green. Instead, she
stopped on the pavement and just stood there, obviously lost in thought.

As usual, although she might be miles away men-
tally, she was turning a few heads, he observed dryly.
Men slowed as they walked past, then looked back.
Girls and women looked too, no doubt marvelling at
the simple elegance of her clothes, the beautiful, lithe
body beneath, the gloss of her skin and hair, maybe
wondering if she was a top model or a film star.

But what the hell has she been doing at Lifeline?
Brett Harcourt wondered. Looking for some new and
devious way to give me the slip? Unless she's decided
to include good works in her repertoire of unusual
activities...

He was about to hail her when he realised the light
had changed and the traffic behind him was getting
restive. He swore beneath his breath and moved off
fast. But he noticed out of the corner of his eye as he
did so that she didn't even look up.

As for Nicola, she came out of her reverie and decided
to treat herself to lunch in town.

She left her car where it was parked and walked to
the Pier, where she chose Pescis, an Italian waterfront
restaurant, overlooking the Marlin Marina. Not that
there was a lot left of the marina. A cyclone earlier
in the year had washed away the pontoons, leaving
only the piles.

But it would be rebuilt, for it had famous associa-
tions, the Marlin Marina, with people like the late Lee
Marvin, who had come to Nicola's home town of
Cairns, in far North Queensland, to set out in pursuit

of the fabulous black marlin in the tropical waters of the Coral Sea.

Pescis was always busy, and today was no exception, but she found a table on the veranda and ordered a light lunch—chopped cooked tomato and basil on toasted bread.

While she waited for it, and sipped mineral water, she fiddled absently with her wedding ring and thought back over her interview with the Reverend Peter Callam—but, more particularly, on the impulse that had made her go in the first place.

I suppose it was because I can never talk to Brett about it, she mused. Not that I've tried for a while, but it always ended up in an argument... I must have been mad...

She looked down at the gold ring on her left hand. It had never been accompanied by an engagement ring—she'd insisted she didn't want one, that it would be a bit ridiculous, because they could hardly call themselves engaged when they were to get married within a bare week of Brett proposing the marriage of convenience quite out of the blue to her. And, finally, weren't engagement rings a token of love?

She'd asked her husband-to-be this with a dangerous little glint in her blue eyes, which he'd observed placidly, then he'd shrugged and murmured that it was up to her. But he'd gone on to say that their wedding would not be a hole-and-corner affair if she had that in mind as well.

'But surely you don't want all the trimmings?' she'd protested. 'I certainly don't.'

'What would you like?' he'd countered. 'Don't forget we need to make some kind of a statement, after what's happened to you and what people are saying.'

'Well...' She'd coloured. 'Something quiet and dignified.'

A look of amusement had flickered in his eyes, causing her to say rashly, 'I'm quite capable of being dignified, Brett.'

'Oh, I believe you, although I sometimes prefer you when you're not, but...' He'd shrugged.

Her eyes had widened—and, she recalled, sitting now on the veranda, watching the green waters of Trinity Inlet, which formed Cairns Harbour, that had given her another cause to hope.

So she'd made no further objections, and she'd married Brett Harcourt in a simple but beautiful, ballerina length dress of ivory stiffened silk, with a matching pillbox hat crowned with flowers, no veil and short gloves. The ceremony had taken place in the garden of his home, before a marriage celebrant, and the handful of guests had all been of his own family. His children had been present, but, at three and four, had had no real idea of the significance of the occasion.

They'd been wild with delight, however, when she'd moved in permanently from that day.

She finished her lunch with a sigh and remembered that, when making her marriage vows, she'd been uncomfortable and barely audible. Then she'd taken hold and told herself that at least she was in love with her tall, worldly husband, so it couldn't all be a sham. But of course now, in hindsight, that was what it still was and always had been.

* * *

'All quiet on the western front?'

'Oh!' Nicola started. It was that evening, and she was seated at a large and beautiful maple desk in the den, dealing with the household accounts. There was an open chequebook in front of her and a sheaf of bills. It was eight-thirty, the children were in bed asleep, Mendelssohn was playing on the state-of-the-art sound system—and she hadn't heard Brett come home.

She pushed a pair of horn-rimmed spectacles up on top of her head and regarded him severely. He had a glass of whisky in one hand and was pulling off his tie with the other. 'You were supposed to be home for dinner.'

'Sorry,' he murmured. 'I got held up.'

'You don't have to apologise to me. Your children are another matter, however. You promised to watch The Wiggles with them.'

'Damn, I forgot.' Brett Harcourt raked his hand through his dark brown hair. 'Don't they put out videos? I could watch a Wiggles video with them.'

'This was a special concert—televised live.'

'So I'm well and truly in the sin bin?'

'I would say so. And you could find yourself in the sin bin with your liver if you make a habit of dining on Scotch.'

Brett Harcourt had hazel eyes that could be extremely enigmatic at times, much to Nicola's chagrin. They could also be coolly insolent and worldly—another thorn in her flesh. But there were times—and she often wondered if she didn't find this the most infuriating—when they laughed at her, although he maintained a perfectly straight face. Such as now.

He said gravely, 'This is my first and last one for the day. It's been a hell of a day and I got my secretary to order some dinner for me. *Have* you taken up good works, Nicola?'

She blinked at him. He sat down on the corner of the desk and let that hazel gaze drift over her. She'd changed into a large white T-shirt printed with gold and silver shells, and a pair of yellow leggings. Her hair was twisted up and secured by a big plastic grip. Her feet were bare. 'What on earth do you mean?'

'You sound as if you're trying to reform me. You even sounded *wifely*, which is something you avoid at all costs, you must admit.'

The slightest tinge of pink ran beneath the smooth skin of her cheeks, but she said coolly, 'With good reason, Brett. I'm a wife in name only, aren't I?'

'How often have you reminded me of that, I wonder?' he murmured, this time smiling openly.

'As often as I try to remind you that you're a *husband* in name only, and that you needn't think you can run my life,' she responded evenly.

'I didn't think I did that.'

Nicola stared at him and tried to mask her impatience, which never worked with Brett.

'Well, do I?' he asked reasonably. 'Tell me about any of your activities I've ever put a stop to. Tell me that you don't come and go as you please, arrange your days as you please—'

'But if I suddenly decided I wanted to go to…Tibet, that would be a different matter, wouldn't it?' she returned tautly.

'Decidedly,' he agreed lazily. 'I don't think that would be a good idea at all.'

She stared at him frustratedly. 'You *know* what I mean.'

'I know we agreed—after you got yourself virtually kidnapped by a man who was a notorious womaniser—that this would be a safer way to go, Nicola.'

'I was only nineteen,' she said through pale lips.

'You're only twenty now—all right—' he shrugged as she opened her mouth to protest '—almost twenty-one. But I can't help wondering whether you've acquired the wisdom you so noticeably lacked then.' His eyes mocked her. 'Wild talk of Tibet doesn't seem to go hand in hand with maturity. And that brings me to something else—what *were* you doing at Lifeline today?'

Nicola gasped. 'How...? He *didn't*!'

'I felt sure there would be a "he" involved,' her husband said dryly.

She jumped up. 'Having a man around is one thing you can't accuse me of, Brett! Since...since it happened—and I had no idea he was going to lure me away under false pretences and all the rest—' she shuddered with disgust '—I haven't had anything to do with men! You make it sound as if I go around inviting their attention.'

Brett Harcourt raised a wry eyebrow. 'You don't have to, Nicola. They attach themselves. So. What's with Lifeline? And why were you looking so very pensive?'

'If you've been having me followed, Brett...' she said through her teeth.

'You'll...?' he queried before she could go on.

The desire to make another wild statement gripped

her, but she fought it, causing his lips to twist as he watched her with interest.

'Were you?' she ground out at last.

'No. I merely happened to be stopped at that particular traffic light as you came out. Now, if you have decided to add good works to your music—' he indicated the beautiful harp that stood in the corner of the den '—your flying lessons, your desire to speak Indonesian and your pottery, I'm all for it—but...' He paused. 'Something tells me it's not so.'

Nicola took a deep breath. 'I do play that harp, I do speak Indonesian, I *love* pottery and I enjoy flying—are you trying to belittle me for any specific reason?' she asked with a quizzically raised eyebrow.

He shrugged, smiled slightly and ignored the question. 'I'm not disputing that. In fact, I'll go further and say that you're highly intelligent as well as artistic, and your flying instructor reckons you're a natural. It still doesn't explain Lifeline.'

Nicola paced around the room and darkly contemplated the fact that it was impossible to hide most things from Brett—it always had been. Which made it rather surprising to think that she'd been able to hide the most important thing of all from him.

She paused beside the harp and ran her fingers gently across the strings in a glissando, to make a golden bell of sound, then stilled it with her palm and turned to look at him.

He was still sitting on the corner of the desk, idly running his tie through his fingers—quite a colourful tie, with red, navy and jade diamonds on it etched in a bone colour that matched his shirt.

But even sitting he was obviously a tall man, who

happened to be twelve years her senior with a mind that was razor-sharp. He also had aquiline features, an impressive build and, although he wasn't precisely handsome, once you got to know him you couldn't help but be aware that he had a rare charm when he chose.

And when he didn't choose there was the aura of a powerful intellect combined with a strong physique that gave notice of a man who got his own way frequently.

All in all an irresistible combination, and not only to me, she thought gloomily. To most women—and, even although they've been divorced for four years, still to Marietta, she suspected...

'Nicola?'

She focused her gaze on her husband and shrugged. 'I went to see a marriage counsellor, that's all.'

It gave her a fleeting sense of satisfaction to see that she had momentarily stunned him. Then he said a shade grimly, 'A man?'

'Yes, he was a man—that threw me at first as well, but—'

'Nicola.'

'But he's also a minister, and he was very nice, Brett, you don't have to worry on that score.'

'And what did he advise you to do?'

'Well, you're *really* going to enjoy this,' she said with simple satire. 'He advised me to stay put.'

For a moment she wondered if her eyes were playing tricks on her, because she could have sworn she saw him relax slightly. Then he said, 'Not what you wanted to hear, I'm sure.'

'No,' she agreed, and shrugged. 'That doesn't mean to say I'll stick to the letter of his advice.'

'Nicola, I—'

'Don't, Brett,' she said with a sudden, weary little gesture. 'I have no plans to go anywhere at the moment, but that doesn't mean to say I'm reconciled to anything.'

He seemed about to say something, then apparently changed his mind and murmured with a humorous little glint, 'So I can expect you to be here for your twenty-first birthday?'

'Yes.' She shrugged.

'You don't sound very enthusiastic.'

'I'm not but I'll probably come round.' She studied *him* unenthusiastically, then a faintly malicious glimmer lit her blue eyes. 'By the way, don't imagine you've escaped The Wiggles.'

'Why not? I mean to say,' he amended hastily, 'I never intended to. I did forget.'

'And then breathed a sigh of relief, no doubt. But we didn't watch them.'

Brett Harcourt looked at his wife narrowly. 'How come?'

'Well, knowing how much you love them, I persuaded your children to let me tape the programme so that we could all watch it together some time tomorrow. Which is a Saturday, in case you've forgotten, and one of the two days of the week you keep inviolate from work or whatever.'

'You—did that to me?'

'Yes, Brett, I did,' she responded gravely, then started to laugh. 'They're very good, you know.'

'If you're a kid. Four young men who've tapped

into the kindergarten set and made a fortune, I imagine,' he said meditatively. 'Oh, well.'

'You could thank me for averting a crisis. Sasha was distraught when you didn't turn up.'

'Sasha is every bit as histrionic as her mother,' Brett Harcourt said a shade grimly.

'And getting more and more like her by the day,' Nicola agreed with a reminiscent little grin.

'How about Chris?'

'Oh, I think he's going to be a chip off the old block.'

He raised an eyebrow at her. 'Me?'

'Yes, you.'

'In what way?'

Nicola considered. 'He's clever—and practical. He said to Sasha, when she was throwing herself on the floor in floods of tears, "Don't be so silly, Sash. If we tape it we can fast-forward all the advertisements."'

Brett chuckled softly. 'Definitely a man after my own heart. What did she say to that?'

'Well, she's no fool either,' Nicola mused with secret laughter lurking in her eyes. 'She said she *liked* the advertisements, they gave you a chance to go and get drinks and things, and she couldn't stand the way men imagined they were driving a speed car when they had a remote control in their hands—flicking from one channel to another, fast-forwarding things and so on.'

'You're kidding. She's only six.'

'All the same, in more juvenile terms, that's what she said! Six is old enough to be struck by male failings, apparently. You, for example, are a nightmare to watch television with for just that reason. So is Chris.'

'Good Lord!'

'So, there you go.' Nicola sat down and pulled the sheaf of bills towards her.

'We've been invited out to lunch on Sunday, by the way,' Brett said after a moment.

'Anywhere interesting? Can we take the kids?'

'Of course. The Masons—I believe you met them at the Goodes' dinner party a few weeks ago.'

Nicola wrinkled her brow. 'Oh, yes, I remember. He's a big, bearded bear of a man and she's small and cuddly and given to being embarrassingly frank.' She looked amused. 'Isn't he the new District Court Judge?'

'The same. They've invited us to their house at Buchans Point. They have a pool as well as the beach. The kids should enjoy it.'

'Sounds nice.' Nicola threw down her pen to yawn heartily. 'I think I'll finish these tomorrow.'

'Tired?' he asked casually as he watched her tuck her feet beneath her.

'I don't know why.'

'The rigours of marriage counselling?' he suggested.

'I think the rigour was on the other foot, if anything.' She grimaced. 'He was quite bemused.'

'Let's hope he's quite discreet,' Brett said.

'He assured me he was.'

Brett stood up and stretched. 'Because I doubt whether you'd enjoy featuring in the gossip columns any more than I would, Nicola.'

They stared at each for a long moment, until he

added, 'Don't forget, that was the other object of this exercise—to protect your fair name from being dragged through the mud.'

'And on that properly grateful note—' she got up and curtseyed '—I'll take myself to bed, sir!'

He said nothing, but his eyes were suddenly cynical and cold.

Don't say it, Nicola warned herself. But, as so often happened, she failed to take her own advice—although she did manage to sound fairly clinical instead of rashly impassioned. 'There are times when I hate you, Brett.'

'I know.' He picked up his glass and drained it.

'Doesn't it ever bother you?'

He set the glass down on the desk, stared at it for a moment, then raised his eyes to hers. There was so much amusement in them now, she caught her breath at the same time as a little frisson ran down her spine. A frisson of awareness that she despised herself for but couldn't help, because Brett Harcourt did that to her even when he laughed at her.

'No, Nicola. You remind me of Sasha, actually. She often hates me when she doesn't get her own way. Why *don't* you go to bed? You not only sound tired and cross, you look it.'

She opened her mouth, then bit her lip and walked past him. But he put out a hand and closed it round her wrist. 'Good thinking,' he said with soft satire, then genuinely laughed at her expression. 'OK, OK, I'm sorry! Of course you don't remind me of Sasha, that was tit for tat, but there is nothing on earth for you to be in a state about.'

They were very close—close enough for Nicola to

see the little golden flecks in his eyes and feel that
frisson of awareness grow into something stronger as
his lean, strong fingers moved on the soft skin of her
inner wrist.

'If you say so, Brett,' she murmured colourlessly,
and removed her gaze from the line of his shoulders
beneath the bone-coloured shirt, hoping and praying
at the same time that he had no idea what the strong
column of his throat and those broad shoulders sometimes did to her—evoking an erotic little desire to
explore them with her fingertips and follow that trail
with her lips.

He released her abruptly. 'I do. Goodnight, Nicola.'

But something stopped her from moving immediately, something that made her look at him fleetingly,
into his eyes, to discover that everything—the amusement and everything else—had been leached from his
expression so that it was like looking at a blank wall.

'Goodnight, Brett,' she said then, quietly and
evenly, and slipped away.

Brett Harcourt stood in the same spot for some moments and wondered, as he'd found himself wondering from time to time over the last two years, if his
wife was essentially naive and genuinely had no idea
how attractive and desirable most men found her.
Because it was true that he couldn't accuse her of
appearing to have much interest in men at all, although he'd been right about her effect on them.

But was it something she still had to grow into? he
mused. Or had this marriage of convenience been
even more successful than he'd thought, from the
point of view of keeping the daughter of a man he'd
admired immensely safe? But safe in an ivory tower?

He stared at nothing for a moment, then shrugged.

CHAPTER TWO

SUNDAY dawned clear and hot, although not nearly so hot as Cairns could get. May was one of the nicest months in the far north of Queensland, Nicola often thought. By May the threat of cyclones had receded, the stingers and box jellyfish were removing their deadly tentacles from beaches and the weather was generally cooler and dryer—if not exactly autumnal by southern standards. Although she'd been brought up in Cairns, there was no doubt the hot steamy summers took their toll.

She walked out onto the veranda and absorbed the view.

Brett Harcourt had built a house at Yorkeys Knob, a northern beach suburb of Cairns dominated by a small, steep and wooded headland—the Knob. He'd built his house on the Knob to take in spectacular views of the ocean, as well as the cane fields, of which he owned a large slice, that stretched inland to the range. Sugar cane was not his only investment. He owned banana and avocado plantations, as well as mango farms—for that matter, so did she.

But it was not the injustice of having her inheritance in someone else's hands until she was twenty-three that was on her mind as she gazed at the view, it was only how lovely it all was that preoccupied her.

Out to sea there were magic reefs and cays, not visible at this distance, but once you'd visited them

they stayed in your mind whenever you looked out.
Michaelmas Cay, Upolo—a lovely little hoop of pale
gold sand in a turquoise sea studded with coral—
Green Island, Arlington Reef, and to the north Batt
and Tongue Reefs, the Low Isles, Agincourt Reef and
many more as the Great Barrier Reef rose from the
depths of the Coral Sea.

Closer to home to the north was Trinity Beach and
Palm Cove on the mainland, then Buchans Point—the
venue for lunch today. And the Range, cloaked in its
dense, dark green foliage, rose majestically behind
them to Kuranda and the Atherton Tablelands.

The other advantage of having a house on the Knob
was the wonderful privacy. The road was actually
above their roof level, and their neighbours were hidden by a glorious tangle of tropical shrubbery: pink,
purple and white bougainvillaea, yellow allamanda
and scarlet poinsettia. There were palm trees and cau-
surinas on the front lawn, and beyond, a sheer drop
down to the sea.

She breathed the clear, sparkling air deeply and
turned to look at the house. Built on two levels in a
mixture of stone, timber and glass, it blended well
with the hillside and made the most of the wonderful
views. The upper level, containing the bedrooms and
where she was now standing, had its own deck around
the front of the house, whilst the lower level opened
onto a paved terrace with an in-ground pool and a
thatched open barbecue pavilion. There were big terracotta pots scattered about, in which Nicola grew
flowering perennials, and some flourishing pandanus
palms.

Louvred doors onto the deck and terrace, as well

as simple cotton blinds, let the air flow through the house as well as giving it a slightly Oriental air. The floors inside were all sealed timber or polished slate, and the rooms were uncluttered to minimise the heat but furnished beautifully, with a mixture of modern and colonial. Curiously, the fact that some of it had been Marietta's doing didn't offend Nicola.

There was also a garden for the children, a shed and a kiln for her pottery, and a shady, secretive courtyard outside the front door that was definitely Oriental in design and a delight to Nicola. More of her pottery pots and most of her statues ended up in it, and she grew herbs, lemon trees in tubs, impatiens, and miniature capsicum and chillies beneath a magnificent tree that was at present a blaze of bloom and spreading a pink carpet on the uneven tiles that surrounded it.

The sight of a small face at her bedroom doorway, which was instantly whisked away, alerted her. She waited a couple of moments, then padded back to her room silently and sneaked up to the bed that now had two still mounds beneath the covers. She fell on the bed, causing screams and loud gurgles of laughter to emanate as the mounds wriggled joyfully and they all ended up in a heap.

'Who's been sleeping in *my* bed?' Nicola demanded, feigning utter surprise.

'You knew, you knew!' Chris, short for Christian, chanted.

'How could she know?' his sister contradicted, coming up for air. 'We didn't make a sound. We didn't even breathe!'

'I bet you she knew—'

'OK.' Nicola gathered them on either side of her and plumped up the pillows. 'Let's not start the day with a fight. How about a song instead? Let's see...'

They sang 'The Teddy Bears' Picnic', then, because The Wiggles were such a hot topic, embarked on one of their songs about a dog that barked all day and night. They sang the chorus with great gusto and much hilarity, alternating from basso profondo to a shrill, scratchy falsetto.

'All right, all right!' Brett Harcourt appeared at the doorway with his hair hanging in his eyes, wearing only a pair of sleep shorts and with blue shadows on his jaw. 'Doesn't anyone in this house believe it's Sunday?'

Nicola said through her laughter, 'Sorry, but they both have perfect pitch, you know!'

Sasha and Chris leapt off the bed to besiege their father, and presently to partake peaceably of a late breakfast, and then get through the whole traumatic business of being dressed and groomed for an outing without one squabble.

'There.' Nicola slung a large bag into the back of the BMW between the children and stood for a moment with her hand on her hip.

She wore a filmy beige and white paisley overshirt and white linen drawstring pants. Her hair was in a simple knot and she had beige canvas rope-soled espadrilles on her feet. She held up a finger for each item. 'I've got two spare sets of clothing, sun-cream, hats, togs, buckets, spades, toys in case they get bored, books—I've got the lot.'

She swung herself into the front seat and exchanged

a wry glance with her husband, who said, 'It's like moving an army.'

'You're not wrong. Now listen, kids,' she said over her shoulder, 'we're going to visit Mr and Mrs Mason for lunch. Don't forget your manners, will you?'

'*I* never do,' Sasha said proudly and pointedly.

''Course you do,' Chris responded. 'Who threw a plate of jelly at—?'

'That was because he pulled my hair! And don't forget the time you *spat* at—'

'Kids,' Brett said, mildly enough, but they subsided—as they always did for Brett, Nicola thought ruefully.

'Wish I had you around more often,' she murmured with a faint grin, and glanced at him expressively.

Gone was the dishevelment of earlier. He was shaved, his brown hair was orderly and he wore a brown and white striped T-shirt, off-white thin cotton jeans and white deck shoes. The hairs on his arms, she noted, glinted chestnut in the sun.

'I might not be so effective then—familiarity could dull the edge.'

'I doubt it. They're always good for you.'

'Do you find them such a handful, Nicola?' he asked after a moment. 'By the way, I presume I'm forgiven?'

'For last night?' She shrugged. 'Yes. You know I don't find them a handful,' she added with more warmth. 'And on the odd occasion that I do,' she said honestly, 'I've always got Ellen to fall back on.' Ellen doubled as housemaid and babysitter, and had been with the children since birth.

'I just wondered,' he said slowly, 'whether they had

anything to do with your seeking counselling. Whether you felt tied down, were yearning for a career or something like that,' he said, before she could speak.

Nicola paused. 'I never could decide whether I wanted to be a potter, a pilot or a musician—that's strange, isn't it? No. It's not that, Brett.'

'But what would you do if you left us?'

The question hung in the air—air that rushed by as they drove up the highway past Palm Cove towards Buchans Point with the roof down. And it was a question that affected Nicola suddenly and curiously. Was it because, she wondered, it was the first time Brett had actually asked her? Not in the context of pointing out her lack of purpose in life, or her unwisdom et cetera, but just as a simple, genuine enquiry?

And it came to her with a little stab of shock that perhaps he was entertaining the idea of her leaving...

'I...I could start my own gallery,' she said at random. 'A lot of people are very taken with my pottery.'

'Anything else?'

She cast around in her mind a little desperately. Before anything presented itself, she remembered suddenly that Brett had gone out the night before, alone, and come home very late. Well after midnight, in fact, as she'd seen on the luminous dial of her bedside clock when the opening and closing of the garage doors had woken her briefly—something she hadn't recalled until now.

Not that there was anything particularly unusual in it. She often went out with girlfriends, and he didn't always include her in his socialising, but...had this been a different kind of socialising, with a woman?

she found herself wondering. A woman he was serious about? Serious enough to be contemplating putting an end to this marriage of convenience. But what about Marietta? she thought. And…

'Nicola?'

She jerked her eyes to his to find his gaze narrow and probing, but all he said was, 'We're here.'

'Oh, sorry.' She shrugged, but it was a long moment before she could tear her gaze away from his. Then she got out of the car and helped the children out.

'Now, let's see.' She straightened Sasha's pretty sun-dress and smoothed her red-brown curls. 'You look gorgeous, darling,' she said, and turned to Chris. 'Whereas you are very handsome, young man!'

Both children exuded gratification and put their hands into hers, leaving their father to deal with the large bag.

And that was what the Masons, Rod and Kim, as well as their resident guest, saw advancing up the garden path as they opened their front door, causing Kim Mason, in her forthright way, to say, 'Nicola, dear, welcome! But how can you possibly be old enough to have two children this age?'

'Oh, she's not our mother,' Sasha piped up with a world-weary air. 'She's our aunt.'

'Sasha.' Nicola frowned down at her. 'I'm not your aunt, I'm your stepmother. Where did you get that idea?'

'Excuse me—how silly of me,' Kim murmured, but Sasha was not to be denied.

'I 'scussed this with my friend Emma, and we decided you can't be any kind of a mother, Nicola, because you don't do the things mummies do.'

''Course she does,' Chris said witheringly. 'Who makes us clean our teeth three times a day and washes our ears and makes us eat our crusts?'

'That's not all mummies do,' Sasha replied with a superior air. 'They look after their kids' dads as well. They kiss and cuddle them, and they sleep in the same bed with them—'

'Sasha,' Brett said from behind a frozen Nicola, 'that'll be enough, thank you.'

'But what would Chris know about it? He's only a silly little boy who doesn't even go to school yet— and that's why we decided, me and Emma, that she's got to be an aunt!' Sasha finished triumphantly.

Instead of falling into a convenient hole that might magically open up at her feet, Nicola had no alternative but to proceed with the day. To pretend as if Sasha had never spoken and ignore the bemusement in their hosts' expressions, until they hurriedly masked it, gracefully acknowledging the introduction of the other guest—a man of about thirty who was visiting the Masons from Sydney and was in some way related to Kim. His name was Richard Holloway.

Brett did the same, and before long they were seated on a shaded terrace beside the pool, with Ellis Beach below them, stretching northward beside a sparkling sea, sipping aperitifs as the children splashed happily in the water.

As if to make up for the incredible revelations she had unwittingly unleashed, Kim talked non-stop to Nicola while the three men talked cricket.

Then, to Nicola's relief, Kim drew her husband away to deal with the barbecue and commanded Richard to replenish everyone's drinks.

Brett said into the sudden silence, 'All right?'

'Yes. No. I had no idea…' Their gazes locked and Nicola found herself going hot and cold again as the truly mortifying thought of people wondering whether she did or didn't sleep with Brett crossed her mind.

'No, Nicola, it's not anything you might be thinking,' he said, and he scanned the tense way she was sitting. She looked lovely enough to tempt any man, he thought, and then also thought, They're probably wondering if I'm mad… 'Because it's not anyone's business but our own,' he added.

'How…how do you know what I was thinking?' she asked.

He smiled a little wryly. 'You looked intensely embarrassed.'

'I felt it—didn't you?'

He shrugged philosophically. 'I'm older and probably tougher. It was also out of the mouths of babes, so to speak.'

'Isn't that a euphemism for an uncanny ability to see the truth? I told you she was no fool.'

'Obviously not,' he said dryly.

'You mustn't be cross with her,' Nicola responded swiftly. 'She doesn't understand the implications of what she said. It's simply something she noticed and found strange.'

'I'm not cross with her. Or only for inheriting her mother's ability to lack any sense of tact or diplomacy.'

Nicola found her lips twisting involuntarily. 'It's

the kind of situation Marietta would enjoy. By the way, when's she due home?'

'When she suffers some pangs of maternal longing, probably,' he said cynically.

Nicola said nothing for a time. Marietta swooped in and out of her children's lives like a brilliant bird of paradise. And, unnatural as it might seem, they adored her when she was around and appeared to accept her absence with equanimity. She had a unit in town, where they went to stay with her to be shamelessly indulged, but they cast it all off like a second skin when they came back to their father.

That they'd only been two and one when the breakup of the marriage had occurred might account for it, Nicola sometimes thought. But it was hard to see why Marietta had bothered to have children, unless Brett had insisted...

Yet, so long as she didn't have to be tied down by them, she was genuinely fond of them. She wrote to them often, rang them from strange places and brought home marvellous exotic gifts for them.

But that's Marietta for you, she thought as she accepted another drink from Richard Holloway. Kim and Rod did not return, so, while the men started discussing politics this time, she was able to think her own thoughts.

She remembered her father's bemusement at Brett's decision to marry Marietta Otway, daughter of his best friend. Brett had been twenty-five, Marietta the same age; Nicola herself had been thirteen.

'Why?' she'd asked her father.

'Well, it's obvious why. She's talented, spirited and *very* beautiful,' he'd said with some irritation.

'So why don't you approve?'

He'd shrugged uneasily. 'You know her. She was babysitting you for pocket money from the time she was sixteen. She's—obsessive, wouldn't you agree?'

'About her music, yes.' Nicola had smiled reminiscently. 'She gave me my first piano lesson when I was four. But—'

'And now she's obsessive about Brett. But I just can't help wondering how marriage is going to fit in with her main obsession—her music.'

Nicola had said slowly, and with no acrimony, 'You look upon Brett as the son you never had, don't you, Dad?'

Her father had ruffled her hair. 'I'm very fond of him and very proud of him. When you think how he had to battle his way through school, let alone law school, despite the Rotary Scholarship—'

'Which you were responsible for.'

'Yes, well, I'd never encountered such a sharp mind before, such a determination to succeed. When his father was lost in a yachting accident at sea he was only twelve, and the oldest of five children, but the support he gave his mother and his younger brothers and sisters was amazing. He was picking mangoes and avocados in his spare time, sorting prawns and so on—but I have only one child dear to my heart, and that's you.'

Two weeks later they'd gone to Brett and Marietta's wedding. At the reception, at a smart restaurant, Nicola had found herself observing the bride and groom with her father's misgivings in mind.

Marietta had been married in a lime-green figure-hugging Thai silk suit that had set off her glorious red hair admirably. She'd glowed, obviously radiantly happy, but, Nicola had noticed, she and Brett had almost steered clear of each other, and Nicola had wondered why.

Then, when they had come together to cut the cake, they'd looked into each other's eyes, and to her teenage eyes it had been as if something white-hot existed between them in that brief glance, something almost dangerous that couldn't be allowed to be exposed in public.

Not long after the wedding Nicola had been sent to boarding school in Brisbane, a thousand miles away, and her dealings with Brett and Marietta had been limited. But she had noticed, when Sasha was born, that Marietta seemed to be obsessive about motherhood in her unique way. Then Chris had arrived, only twelve months later, and after another twelve months had come the bombshell that Brett and Marietta were separating.

'I knew it,' her father had said exasperatedly.

'But Chris is only a baby! How can she?'

'They've come to an agreement. The children will spend the bulk of their time with Brett, allowing her the licence to get her career back on track,' he'd said sardonically.

'But I thought she liked having children.'

'It was a novelty, that's all.'

Nicola had thought deeply. By then seventeen, she'd had more of an understanding of that strange, searing little look she'd intercepted between Brett and Marietta on their wedding day, but she'd found herself understanding this turn of events even less. 'So don't they love each other any more?'

Her father had sighed. 'They may do, but she's determined to have it on her terms or not at all, and Brett... Well, he didn't get where he is without his own kind of iron determination.'

By this time Brett had been made a partner in her father's law firm. Indeed, he was the active partner, whose expertise had brought some big and prestigious clients to act for, and her father was coming to rely on him more and more as his health failed.

At eighteen Nicola had left boarding school, and, because of her father's poor health, she insisted on spending the last six months of his life as his constant companion, instead of starting a Bachelor of Arts degree as she'd planned. This had brought her into close contact with Brett and his children—Brett had been marvellous, right up to the end and beyond.

And she often thought it was during those sad months that she'd fallen in love with Brett Harcourt. But it was on the understanding that what was between him and Marietta was not resolved, and that somehow things would be patched up.

She'd spent a lot of time with his children, though, during the restless months after her father's death, often staying with them rather than rattling around home alone. She had done this not only on his account, but the children's, and Marietta's too. It had been like having two warring members of her own family around, both of whom she loved.

She couldn't forget all the years she'd known Marietta. Could never forget how Marietta had flown home for her father's funeral to play some of his favourite pieces. They had brought him so vividly to mind, yet in the way they'd been played—so exquisitely and gently—had laid him to rest in her heart, even though she still suffered, and had no idea what she wanted to do with her suddenly empty life.

Brett had suggested university again, but she hadn't wanted to commit herself. She wasn't even sure whether she'd agreed to a Bachelor of Arts in the first place only to please her father. She'd suggested an overseas trip, but Brett had vetoed it, saying she was too young to go on her own. That was when she'd first discovered that she might love Brett Harcourt, but it didn't prevent her from being in discord with him...

Indeed, that was what she'd thrown at him after she'd drifted into company with a fast set of so-called friends—another cause for disagreement between them—and, without quite understanding how, had got herself so embarrassingly compromised by a man of whom, ever since, the mere thought made her shudder.

It had all been so trite and sordid.

A party of them had been going up to the Tablelands for a long weekend, or so she'd been led to think. But no one else had turned up, and she'd found herself alone, in a remote cabin, fending off the distinctly amorous and then frighteningly violent attentions of a man who called her a rich, spoilt little bitch and speculated that she was Brett Harcourt's mistress—she certainly spent enough time at his house, and it was already the subject of some comment around town, wasn't it?

Nicola had suddenly been more horrified than frightened, and this had given her the momentum to slap his face, then storm off proudly when he'd drawled that she'd have to find her own way home.

That was something she hadn't been able to do without calling on Brett for help when she'd finally found a phone.

The interview that had followed as he'd driven her back to Cairns had been deadly. How could she have been such a fool? Hadn't he warned her about the company she was keeping and the men she was going out with? What did she think she looked like, wandering around the countryside dusty and dishevelled with her dress torn?

That was when she'd thrown the idea of an overseas trip at him in her anger and shame.

He'd driven her straight to Yorkeys Knob, but as he'd been about to get out of the car she'd swallowed suddenly and said, 'No, not here...please.'

'Why?'

'I just can't.' But her face had burned, and something in the way she'd refused to look at him had made him pause. Then he'd said unemotionally that he'd take her home and had done so. Only once there he'd proceeded to insist on being told everything. But, instead of being shocked and disgusted by the news of the kind of gossip they were the subject of, he'd merely said that she should have a shower and get changed because he planned to take her out to dinner.

And it had been over dinner, when she was much calmer and no longer feeling such a fool, that he'd proposed marriage—of a kind.

She could still remember the blue linen tablecloth and the steady flame of a candle in a glass, the music in the background and the dress she'd worn—black with white flowers, a high little mandarin collar and a row of pearl buttons down the front. Her hair had been lying on her shoulders, clean and slightly fluffy because she hadn't had time to dry it properly.

She remembered the half-eaten butterfly prawns she'd ordered, the glass of wine she'd been toying with. And her first shocked response—'*What about Marietta?*'

He smiled dryly. 'That's all over. Didn't you know?' He looked at her ironically.

'But is that why it's only to be a—a fake marriage?'

'No. It's because you're too young to be marrying anyone, Nicola, but at least this way you'll be able to be comfortable and happy, and doing something you obviously enjoy.'

She picked up her wine glass, then looked challengingly at him over the rim. 'Taking care of your children?'

'Marietta's too. And it's not that I'll expect you to be a babysitter-cum-governess,' he went on. 'You can do whatever you like, but with you there they're happy, and so are you. Aren't you?'

'Yes. But for how long?'

He shrugged. 'As long as it seems necessary. You could even do a part time university course if you wanted to. And if it doesn't appeal to you—well, at least you'll know you've given it a shot.'

'You sound like my father.'

He said nothing for a long moment, then added, 'It is something he would have wanted you to do. By the way, Nicola, it would be an honour to have you gracing my house.'

Her eyes widened, and that was when the first rash seed of hope sprouted. But she immediately cautioned herself against believing anything. 'Just say you fall in love, or I fall in love—tomorrow, for example.' She gestured.

'I don't think that's liable to happen to me, but I promise to tell you if it does,' he said gravely. 'And if it happens for you, I still think you should wait a while before you allow yourself to believe it's the love of your life.'

She shrugged and chewed her lip, then, with the first glint of humour in her eyes for quite a while, said, 'At the moment I'm thoroughly turned off men, believe me. But—' she frowned '—just say it did happen—mightn't it complicate things incredibly? Having to explain that I am married but not really, kind of thing, let alone having to go through annulments and whatever?'

'Not for a man who really loves you, no.'

She blinked, then heard herself saying, 'I don't know what else to do. I feel like a ship without a rudder. I suppose because I was an only child and I don't even remember my mother…that's why…' She sighed. 'We used to do so much together, Dad and I. We'd planned to go overseas together when I finished school.'

'I know. I envied you.'

'Did you?' For some reason it came as a surprise, and she studied him curiously. He'd left his work to rescue her, and still wore a pale green long-sleeved shirt, fawn trousers and a dark red tie with little green elephants on it. He looked so much a man of the world, so quietly assured and in command, it was hard to imagine him envying her in any way, let alone proposing marriage to her.

She said suddenly, 'I think my father looked upon you as the son he never had. He denied it, but it was true, all the same.' She took a sip of wine, then twirled the glass in her fingers.

'You didn't mind?' He watched her narrowly.

'No. What do you think he'd have made of this, though?' She returned his gaze steadily.

'I think, Nicola…' he said, and paused. 'I think he'd rest easily to know we'd devised a way of getting you through these difficult years—and they can be difficult years for anyone, not least for someone as alone in the world as you are—safely and happily.'

'All the same, it's fraud of a kind,' she murmured a little dryly, and formed her slender hands into a steeple on the table. 'Although it remains to be seen whether we fool anyone.' And there was that glint of challenge in her deep blue eyes again.

'They may draw their own conclusions, but—' he smiled slightly, a cool twisting of his lips that was curiously intimidating '—I can assure you they'd think twice about expressing them, let alone treating you with anything but respect.'

Her brows rose. 'You sound quite formidable, Brett.'

He said nothing, only looked lazily amused, but if anything that reinforced her growing understanding that he *was* formidable when he wanted to be.

'Uh…' She hesitated. 'There is one person who might be entitled to express all sorts of reservations on the subject—they are her children, too.'

'Leave Marietta to me,' he said evenly.

'But I think I should know whether you intend to tell her the truth or not, Brett?'

'Marietta waived certain rights, Nicola, when she walked out on her children, but, if it's OK with you, all I would do is present her with a *fait accompli*. I can't see her not being delighted to have you there for Sasha and Chris.' He raised an eyebrow at her. 'Is that a yes?'

Coming back to the present, with Sasha and Chris still splashing happily in the pool, Brett and Richard Holloway now onto golf, and the aroma of burnt meat wafting across the terrace at Buchans Point, Nicola grimaced to think that she should have been so naive. Because of course she'd not only said yes, but spent the first year of their marriage still hoping for Brett's love, despite going out of her way never to give herself away.

But he'd been right about one thing. No one had cast any aspersions on their marriage openly, or treated her with any reservations or plain mockery.

So, it was really ironic, she thought, that sunny Sunday morning, that it should have been Sasha, his own daughter and a little girl of barely six, who had articulated to the world the state of their marriage.

'My dear!' Kim arrived back, looking hot and bothered. 'I'm sorry, you must have wondered whether we had to slaughter the beast as well as cook its steaks, but Rod is so unhandy with the barbecue. Would you believe, he couldn't get it hot enough? Then it went out, then it was too hot, but lunch is ready.'

'Smells wonderful,' Nicola said consolingly, but untruthfully. 'I'll round up the kids.'

After lunch, and a suitable period to allow it to digest, their hosts suggested that the younger members of the party might like to climb down the hill for a walk along the beach. And when Brett and the children lagged behind, to build sandcastles, Nicola found herself striding out beside Richard Holloway, who said humorously, 'Do you ever regret eating a large, indigestible meal in the middle of the day?'

Nicola glanced at him and her lips quivered. 'They tried so hard. I'm only amazed Sasha or Chris didn't make some remark. Tact is not their—' She stopped abruptly.

'So I gathered,' he said quietly.

A rush of colour prickled the skin of her cheeks, but she held her head high and walked even faster.

Richard Holloway kept up easily. He was lean and rangy, with fair hair and grey eyes. Over lunch he'd been good company, as they'd hacked their way through overcooked steaks and some pointed remarks had flown between the new District Court Judge and his wife. In fact, it had been due to Richard and Brett and the way they'd held the conversation that the little domestic contretemps the Masons were suffering had been defused.

'I'm sorry,' he said. 'Talk of tactless—that was extremely so.'

There was a breeze getting up and stirring the hot sand. Nicola squinted as an extra strong gust swirled the sand head-high, and turned around. 'How long are you staying with the Masons, Mr Holloway?'

'Just for the time being, until I find a place of my own, although Kim assures me I can stay for good,' he replied a little ruefully as they walked back towards Brett and the children. 'I'm working on a commission for a new shopping centre—a centrepiece for the main foyer that combines reef and rainforest, a little bit of the Daintry and coral, et cetera—all the things Cairns is famous for.'

Nicola slowed her pace. 'Are you an artist?'

'I'm a bit of a jack of all trades. I paint, and I sculpt, but when I realised I wasn't going to set the world on fire there, I went in for this kind of design work.'

Nicola looked at him with more interest, and decided he might be a bit younger than her first estimate—twenty-sevenish, perhaps—and that he was also nice.

'I believe you're a potter?' he said then.

'Who told you that?'

'Kim. She said you mentioned it when you first met. Ever done any commercial work? Because I'm looking for some pottery as it happens.'

A little pulse of excitement ran through Nicola's veins, although she said wryly, 'I might not be good enough.'

'You never know. Would it be possible to have a look?'

'I don't see why not,' she said slowly, and was suddenly amazed to have the Reverend Peter Callam in her mind's eye. No, she thought, I'd never do it. But then again, if Brett *was*...if... 'Do you have a wife and family tucked away down south, Mr Holloway?'

He laughed. 'No, I'm not married. Why?'

'No reason,' Nicola said lightly and untruthfully as they came up to Brett and the children. 'Guess what?' she said to Brett. 'I could become employed, after all.'

CHAPTER THREE

BRETT squinted up at her.

He was liberally coated with sand—he'd changed into a pair of green board shorts and a white T-shirt for the expedition to the beach but he'd now taken the T-shirt off, and the muscles of his back and shoulders ran smooth and powerful beneath his lightly tanned skin.

He'd had a swim with the children, and his brown hair hung damp and sandy in his eyes. But Nicola could still see the narrowed, less than impressed expression in them.

'Employed?'

She smiled coolly at him. 'Don't sound so surprised. Mr Holloway will explain.'

Richard Holloway did, enthusiastically.

'Of course, he'll have to see if I'm any good,' Nicola added at the end of it.

'Of course.' Brett stood up, which immediately provoked a protest from Sasha, but he swung her up into his arms then sat her on his shoulders, causing her to assume a regal air. 'Home, Miss Harcourt,' he said, and glanced at Richard and Nicola. 'If that's all right with everyone?'

'Fine with me,' Richard responded, and picked up Chris to sit him on his shoulders. 'We could even make a race of it.'

They did, to the children's delight, leaving Nicola

to follow in their footsteps weighed down with buckets, spades, discarded clothing—and some annoyed thoughts on her mind. But she didn't give expression to them until later that evening.

Sasha and Chris were in bed and asleep by seven o'clock, after a light supper, and Nicola spent the next hour tidying up. Sunday was one of Ellen's days off. She ironed Sasha's school clothes, polished her shoes and prepared as much of her lunch as she could beforehand. She rinsed all the sandy clothes and put them in the washing machine, as well as rinsing off the buckets and spades and storing them.

Brett had taken a phone call during supper, then retired to his study. Or so she'd thought. But when she strolled out onto the terrace with a cup of coffee, she found him relaxing on a lounger, staring into space. It was a starry night, and the heat of the day still lingered in the air—the breeze had died completely.

She paused, then said, 'Thought you were working. Would you like a cup of coffee?'

He had his hands folded behind his head, and he turned slightly to run his hazel gaze over her. She'd changed into a cool, floral voile dress, sleeveless and strapless and gathered onto an elastic band above her bosom and around the waist. A gold locket nestled in the hollow at the base of her throat.

'No, thanks.'

Nicola moved to another lounger and sat down, placing her mug carefully on the deck. 'Then would you care to explain why you were about as enthusiastic as a dead fish earlier?'

'About this pottery thing?'

'Yes,' she said genially. 'That thing. But I should warn you, Brett, I'm going to do it. If I'm good enough.'

'I don't imagine that'll be a problem.'

She frowned. The underwater lights in the pool were on, and there was enough light spilling from the lounge behind them for her to see that after that first comprehensive glance he hadn't looked at her again. 'What's that supposed to mean—that you don't believe I'm much good? As a potter?'

'On the contrary, I do believe you're good. I'm just not sure if that's the criteria.'

'What criteria did you have in mind?' she asked after a moment, with dangerous restraint.

'Nicola,' he said gently but lethally, 'you're no fool, my dear—or you shouldn't be by now. Richard Holloway was not only struck by you—he could barely take his eyes off you—but his curiosity was no doubt pleasurably activated at discovering we are not man and wife in the true sense of the words.'

Nicola took hold of the sheer indignation that had bubbled up to say, with amusement, although that was far from what she was feeling, 'Sprung—and by Sasha of all people. That's rather ironic, isn't it, Brett?'

'Possibly.'

'I take it you don't see the funny side of it now?'

'No, Nicola,' he replied deliberately. 'Nor did you at the time.'

'You're right.' She chewed her lip. 'It was a bit like being pole-axed. You know, you could have a problem there, Brett. When she makes the connection that her father doesn't sleep with her stepmother *or* her mother.'

He was silent.

Nicola moved restlessly, then said, 'What's wrong with Richard Holloway? Unless you imagine he's liable to run off with me?'

Brett stood up and prowled over to the edge of the pool with his hands shoved into his pockets. 'Nothing,' he said at last. 'Nothing that I know of at this stage.' He turned and looked down at her. 'Would you like to get to know him better, Nicola?'

She was sitting sideways on the lounger, with her hands on her knees, and it was a moment before she raised her eyes to his. 'I would like to be gainfully employed, Brett, if for no other reason than to see if it raises me in your estimation at all. And, *yes*, he seems rather nice.'

Her gaze was steady, but his lingered on the locket at her throat, her slim, bare shoulders and slender arms before he looked into her eyes. 'So,' he said, 'the period of being turned off men has ended?'

If only you knew, she thought, and her hands tightened on her knees briefly. 'Perhaps. You surely can't object?' she added huskily.

He looked at her dryly. 'No. All the same, I think we should employ some discretion.'

'Oh, I'd be quite discreet,' she responded. 'But I have to tell you I find your attitude inexplicable. This has blown up out of nothing. I only met the man today, and so far my only intention is to see if I'm a good enough potter to be commercial.'

'So you'll have a career to go to when our marriage ends?'

'Brett.' She discovered her heart was beating strangely. 'I can't spend the rest of my life looking after your children. Can I?'

He didn't answer, but continued to watch her thoughtfully. In fact, the way he looked at her was curiously as if he was summing her up, judging her on a scale of one to ten, trying to see her as other men might see her.

She swallowed and looked away. She felt her nerve-ends tingle, and she wondered whether her filmy dress was any barrier to those probing hazel eyes. Would Brett do that to her? Undress her with his eyes, even if only to assess what her level of desirability would be to other men?

The thought that followed was worse, as she wondered whether she was giving off any unconscious indication that she sometimes yearned for his touch on her skin—when she wasn't hating him, that was. Such as now, with his dispassionate survey of her.

I *can't* go on like this, she thought torturedly. Hating him, loving him, wanting him, and now this ridiculous ploy of trying to make him jealous. Not that I've done anything except agree to show my work to a man who could be interested—until I was goaded into saying I'd like to get to know him better. But *why* is he goading me...?

She sat up suddenly, and clasped her hands.

'What?' Brett said quietly. He'd changed back into his brown and white T-shirt and cotton jeans, but it didn't matter what he wore. There was always the attraction of that strong, lean body, those clever eyes, but...

No, she thought chaotically, he couldn't be jealous.

Surely he'd have given some indication by now—surely he would have. So why was he so disapproving? And why, this morning in the car, had he sounded different, almost as if he was giving some thought to ending this marriage?

'I don't understand, that's all,' she said, barely audibly.

'Your father,' he said abruptly, 'would have been just as—cautious, Nicola, about granting or withholding his approval.'

Her eyes widened.

'So, perhaps I should just say this. You're going to inherit an estate worth a couple of million dollars, you're extremely attractive, but...' he paused, and their eyes locked '...but you're still very young. Don't rush into anything. Not even to get away from me.'

Her breath escaped with a sibilant little sound. So that was it—he was still standing in for her father. She said expressionlessly, 'And when do you think you'll be able to stop acting in *loco parentis*, Brett?'

He was silent for so long she thought he wasn't going to answer. She listened to the waves breaking at the base of the Knob and heard a fruit bat chitter in a mango tree. Then he said, with a slight shrug, 'We could have a re-evaluation after your birthday.'

'You think a week or two is going to make much difference?'

He smiled faintly. 'Who knows? In the meantime, bearing my words of wisdom in mind, why don't you invite Richard Holloway to dinner on Tuesday night? I've invited Tara Wells, and we'll have the Masons too. You could show him your pottery at the same time.'

Nicola wrinkled her brow. 'Tara Wells? Do I know her?'

'No. I had dinner with her on Saturday night. She's just joined the firm. She's moved up here from Brisbane and I imagine she's feeling a bit lost and lonely at the moment.'

'A solicitor?'

'Yes,' he agreed. 'A litigation specialist. I think you'll like her.'

'A formal dinner?' she said slowly, but with her mind far from slow.

'If you like. You do them rather well.'

'Thank you. But isn't it a little early to be inviting the Masons back?'

'I'm sure they won't mind—it could even reassure them that today wasn't an entire debacle.'

She looked briefly amused. 'All right, I'll ring the Masons tomorrow to thank them and invite them at the same time. Why not?' But she stopped to ponder why she suddenly seemed to have lost interest in her pottery.

'As for Sasha, I think we should just ignore the subject,' he said wryly.

Nicola raised an eyebrow. 'I wasn't proposing to go into detailed explanations. But ignore it until the next time she embarrasses us do you mean?'

'She was led into it, somewhat.'

Nicola grimaced, then stood up. 'I never did finish the household accounts. Goodnight.'

'Nicola—' He stopped.

She turned back to him and waited politely.

'I...' He paused and examined her courteous bearing, which barely overlaid something much more taut and wound up. 'I do have your best interests at heart.'

'So you say, Brett. I'll take your word for it. Goodnight.' She was about to sweep indoors when he stopped her again.

'What now?' she queried coolly.

'Two things,' he responded, a little dryly. 'Don't forget the law society ball next Saturday night, and that tomorrow we've been invited to attend an open day at my old high school. You,' he reminded her, 'are to present the achievement award I donate annually.'

Nicola said something unprintable beneath her breath, because she'd forgotten both events. 'Why me? Surely you can do it on your own?'

'I'm making the speech. All they want you to do is hand over the prize. If you recall, you made quite a hit last year.'

'I can't imagine why,' she murmured.

'I can tell you. All the girls saw you as a vision of grace and loveliness and dignity to emulate, and all the boys—were watering at the mouth.'

'Brett, that's—' But she stopped in time, because he was laughing silently at her outraged expression.

'Not so far from the truth, actually,' he murmured, then raised an eyebrow at her. 'You'll come? They'll be so disappointed if you don't.'

Nicola ground her teeth. 'And that's blackmail if ever I heard it—yes, I'll come, but under duress.' And this time she did sweep inside.

Leaving Brett Harcourt to watch her until the house

swallowed her up, then swear beneath his breath as he turned to scan the dark sea.

Sleep didn't come easily that night.

So much so that Nicola got up and had a shower, merely for the soothing benefit of warm water running down her body. Then she chose a fresh, crisp cotton nightgown, smoothed the bed and got back into it to lie on her back with her ankles crossed and her hands clasped behind her head.

You know what I think? she mused to herself. I think the old order is about to change, even if he won't give his approval on my father's behalf to an involvement with a man. And I'm deadly afraid this Tara Wells might be the cause of it. What a name…conjures up Sadlers Wells or Bath and Wells or Scarlett O'Hara. But why else would he suddenly, this morning, after having dinner with her last night, sound as if he could entertain the thought of us parting?

But how doubly ironic, she mused, and sat up abruptly to blow her nose and dab her eyes, that— now it could be about to happen—to be set free, what I thought I wanted, is not going to be what I want at all…

'See what I mean?' Brett said softly, for her ears alone the next morning. She'd just presented his achievement award and sat down on the dais to extremely enthusiastic applause.

It was a warm, shimmering day. She wore a short-sleeved linen suit, with a short skirt in a chalky violet, a huge hat with a curved down brim and a confection of tulle and violet and pale grey flowers around the crown, with matching patent pale grey shoes and purse.

She'd purchased this stunning ensemble to wear to the Cairns Amateurs, a premier racing event in the state, let alone Cairns, and had been worried that it was too dressy when Brett had suggested it, but he'd only murmured, 'The dressier the better.' And it seemed he'd been right. It was certainly finding favour with the students of his old school.

It also found favour with the headmaster and his wife, when they shared a table with them in a marquee on the sports oval. 'We very much appreciate your doing this, Mrs Harcourt, and with such style,' the headmaster said earnestly. 'It's so easy, in this tropical climate especially, to get lazy over matters of dress, and then matters of mind, and the finer things in life generally. But your presence helps to make this day special.'

But in Brett's car on the way home—Nicola had offered to drive herself, so he could go straight on to work after the presentation, but he'd said they'd go together and leave together—she took her hat off and put it over on the back seat, and said gloomily, 'Now I feel a real fraud.'

Brett turned his head to study her briefly as her hair blew out behind her like a pale gold silk scarf.

'I mean, I've done nothing to earn that kind of admiration,' she added.

He stopped at a traffic light and slid one arm along the back of her seat. 'Why don't you just consider yourself as—one of the finer points of life?' he suggested with a little glint of wicked amusement. 'Not to mention a distinct asset to a man,' he said gravely.

'Of course, that's the other reason I feel a fraud,' she commented.

'Are we getting back to the wife-in-name-only discussion, Nicola?' He withdrew his arm and set the car in motion as the light changed.

'It seems fairly topical.' She gazed steadily ahead. 'It's hardly a proper marriage.'

'You do have a tendency to bring it up, I agree.'

Nicola hesitated, then glanced at him. He wore a beautifully tailored charcoal suit, white shirt and discreet green and black tie, and it occurred to her as she studied his aquiline features, his breeze-ruffled thick brown hair and his lean hands on the wheel, that *he* could be described as one of the finer things in life.

And all of a sudden she felt guilty, because—whatever might be between them—this occasion represented not only what he'd achieved with his life but his desire to help others, to put something back. His speech, not in the least condescending but encouraging and amusing, had earned as much applause as she had...

She sighed suddenly, and rested her head against the back of the seat. 'Sorry.'

'What for?' he asked dispassionately.

'For being—well, churlish about today. You may not realise it, but, all else aside, I'm very proud of you, Brett. And so would my father be today.'

They'd flashed up the Knob as she said all this, and now he drew up in front of the house. Nicola opened her door before he could speak, and got out. Then she leant over and retrieved her hat. 'I just didn't want you to think I was so wrapped in myself that I couldn't appreciate what you've done.'

'Nicola...' He said it with a mixture of exasperation and something she couldn't quite define—almost as if he didn't know how to go on. Indeed, his gaze wandered over her, so slender and regal in her beautiful suit, and he shook his head, then opened his mouth.

But her lips curved, and she murmured, 'There— I've surprised you, Brett. Why don't we just leave it at that? See you tonight.' And she walked down the drive, swinging her hat in her hand.

It was a moment before Brett put the car into gear again, and he found himself thinking, You lovely, captivating, unique child—what *am* I going to do with you?

'Reef and beef, Ellen—how does that sound?' Nicola said that afternoon. 'For this dinner party tomorrow night, I mean.'

Ellen, in her fifties and a widow, but spry and bird-like, and with the energy of a small dynamo, cocked her head. 'My brother's due in tomorrow morning. I'm sure I could get some fresh squid off him.'

Her brother was a trawlerman, in fact it was on his trawler that Brett had worked as a teenager, as a deck hand and prawn-sorter in his spare time. And that was how a bond had been forged with Ellen's family, and how Ellen had come to think the sun shone out of Brett Harcourt.

'Calamari,' Nicola said with deep satisfaction. 'Especially the way you do it, Ellen. The perfect entrée!

Then I thought of Beef Wellington and...' she tapped a pencil against her chin '...a mocha mousse?'

'You do have a light hand with a mousse,' Ellen commented. 'Drat that child!'

'What's he done now?' Nicola asked resignedly.

Chris deeply resented being left at home while Sasha went to school, although he did attend a kindergarten—baby school, as Sasha called it—three mornings a week.

'I knew he couldn't have eaten his mashed potato, although it was gone from his plate and him looking all angelic. He put it in my shoe! I slipped them off while I washing the floor.'

Nicola looked around to see whether Chris was in earshot, but there was no sign of him, and she started to giggle helplessly. Ellen, after a moment, joined in, although she said, 'Just wait until I get my hands on him!'

'I wonder if his father was as naughty?'

'More likely he got it from his mother,' Ellen said darkly. She'd never forgiven Marietta for leaving Brett—if that was how it had happened.

'Here, I'll clean it for you.' Nicola picked up the shoe and began, distastefully, to fork mashed potato out of it. 'You know, I'm thinking we should enrol him for something. Something physical.'

'To tire him out? Good idea. Just don't try judo or anything like that. He'll be throwing us around the place before you know it.'

'No.' Nicola grinned. 'But he is good with a ball. Maybe tennis lessons? Do they teach five-year-olds tennis? I'll see what Brett thinks. OK. Back to this dinner party tomorrow night. I really want it to be special.'

Ellen glanced at her affectionately. 'They always are. You have a touch of class. But why this one particularly?'

Nicola chewed her lip. If anyone was in a position to know what a sham their marriage was, Ellen was it, although she didn't live in with them. But she never made any comment.

'I...' Nicola hesitated. 'I just have the feeling I need to be on my mettle tomorrow night, that's all.'

'All right, I'll make a bargain with you two. You can watch The Wiggles concert again provided you go straight to bed after you've said hello to the visitors—and *stay* in bed,' she said the next evening.

'What if I'm dying of thirst or want to go to the bathroom?' Sasha queried. The children were roaming around her bedroom as she did her hair and make-up. Brett hadn't arrived home yet.

'You can go to the bathroom first and take a glass of water to put on your bedside table, Sash. Chris, don't do that.'

'Yuk.' Chris put the perfume atomiser down. 'Why do you want that stuff all over you? And why're you rolling your hair up like that? It looks better down.'

Nicola paused in front of the mirror. She'd been arranging her hair in a neat, elegant and sophisticated pleat at the back of her head, but she studied herself critically. 'Do you really think so?'

''Course I do. Only old ladies wear their hair like that.'

'Oh.' She pulled the pins out and let her hair flow down her back. 'Is that better?'

'Much better,' another voice said—Brett's.

'See!' Chris said triumphantly, and rushed to hug his father. It was a few moments before they realised why Sasha hadn't done likewise—she had liberally and inaccurately painted her lips bright scarlet.

Nicola groaned, and reached for some cleanser and a tissue. 'Really, Sash! That won't come off as easily as it goes on. It's like getting dressed with an army of—I don't know what!'

'I'll take them off your hands,' their father said ruefully.

Ten minutes later, Nicola looked into the den to see them all watching television peacefully, and with a sigh of relief she went to put the finishing touches to her table.

The formal lounge and dining area were one big room in the house on the Knob. A lovely old refectory table dominated the dining area, and tonight it was set with cream linen place mats, her own blue-glazed pottery candlesticks and an ivory porcelain dinner service. There was a low bowl of pink Cooktown orchids between the tall candlesticks.

Satisfied with the table, Nicola inspected the lounge area, plumping up some cushions on the oatmeal linen-covered settees, and the three jewel-bright velvet-covered chairs—one jade-green, one topaz-yellow and one Ming-blue. She adjusted the occasional tables and switched on some lamps, dimming the overhead light.

Finally she looked around, and nodded.

'Satisfied?' Brett said from behind her.

'Yes. Are—?'

'They're fine; they've sworn to be on their best behaviour. I've had a shower, and I think you deserve a drink in the peace and quiet of the next fifteen minutes before everyone arrives.' He handed her a sherry.

Surprise made Nicola arch an eyebrow, but she took it with murmured thanks.

'Sit down,' he suggested. He'd changed into a fresh blue and white pinstriped shirt and navy trousers.

A glint of humour lit her eyes as she sank into the Ming chair. 'I must be looking frazzled.'

'Not at all.' He sat down opposite her. 'You're looking very beautiful.' His gaze lingered on her short, straight black dress, with its narrow trim of ivory satin around the neckline, armholes and hem. She wore a five-strand pearl bracelet, pearls in her ears and high, slender black sandals.

He glanced down the length of her legs, then studied her hair in its fair, smooth sweep to below her shoulders, and finally looked into her eyes, with amusement evident in his own. 'Do you always take Chris's advice on your appearance?'

'He's the only male I've got to go by. Strangely enough, he's often right. Perhaps he gets his taste from you?'

'Do you think I have good taste when it comes to women?'

Nicola chewed her lip and regretted saying anything on the subject. 'Marietta was—is—very beautiful,' she mused thoughtfully, though after a slight pause.

He watched her meditatively for a moment, then, 'Marietta and I were violently attracted to each other. But I think we should have known better.' He shrugged.

Nicola frowned. 'That's a strange thing to say. I don't—understand.'

'Well, it was very difficult to handle, even without the pressures of children, and her and my own dedication to our careers.'

'But you did love her, didn't you?'

'I thought so at the time, Nicola,' he said quietly. 'But, whatever it was, it literally burnt itself out.'

Nicola blinked several times. 'Why are you telling me this, Brett?'

'Because I don't think you've ever believed it's over between us.'

'No, I haven't,' she said honestly. 'And, if you must know, I really think that between you you could have had more sense than to have not one but two children to inherit the burden of—' she gestured '—a broken marriage.'

He stared down at the glass in his hands, then grimaced. 'Hindsight is a very valuable commodity. But, if you look at it another way, mightn't we be poorer without Chris and Sasha in our lives?'

Nicola stared at him and went quite pale. 'Of course,' she said, and closed her eyes. 'Why did I say that?'

He smiled faintly. 'Not because you don't love them enough—even to considering yourself as their guardian angel, Nicola. Don't look like that. And, as unwise as we may have been, Marietta and I, these things do happen. But I'm doing my level best not to let it affect them too much.'

'So what happens when I'm gone?' she asked abruptly.

He stood up, took her glass, and the front doorbell rang. 'I would continue to have their best interests at heart, Nicola. Our guests have arrived.'

Talk about your *mythical mistresses*, Reverend Callam, Nicola found herself thinking at one stage, during what turned out to be a very long evening. If Tara Wells hasn't got her sights on Brett, I'm a Dutchman! *Is* that what it's all about?

But, before she'd got to that stage, she'd welcomed their guests warmly, and Sasha and Chris had come out to be introduced, and to reacquaint themselves with the Masons and Richard Holloway. Nicola had discovered she was holding her breath in case Sasha let out any more household secrets, but she and Chris had behaved beautifully, looking so angelic in their pyjamas and dressing gowns it was hard to equate them with the secreting of mashed potato in shoes, for example.

Then Ellen had come to take them to bed and Nicola had breathed a sigh of relief, at the same time catching a wicked little glint of amusement in Brett's eye.

It was Tara Wells who'd said whimsically, 'How adorable—but then I'm told that's the best time to view children, just before they go to bed.'

Everyone had laughed, and as Brett handed out champagne cocktails Nicola had taken a moment to study this guest about whom she had such grave doubts.

Tara Wells was about thirty, tall, slender and dark, with pale, perfect skin and beautiful green eyes. She wore a dove-grey silk suit with short sleeves, and no jewellery other than a large gold wristwatch on a black alligator band—there were no rings on either hand. And she undoubtedly had a presence. You could easily see her being a quiet force to be reckoned with in a court of litigation.

You could also see appreciation of another kind in the eyes of both Richard Holloway and Rod Mason, and a little spurt of annoyance in Kim Mason's eyes as she observed her husband being courtly and deferential towards Tara Wells. Oh, no, Nicola thought, not another cause for dispute between the District Court Judge and his wife?

But it was towards Nicola herself that Tara displayed the most interest. She said, just before dinner was served, 'Brett's told me all about you, Nicola, but even he didn't do you justice.'

'Why, thank you,' Nicola heard herself respond with caution—due, she discovered a moment later, to a feeling of discomfort to think of Brett discussing her with anyone. Why should they be discussing her anyway? 'I'm afraid he hasn't told me anything about you,' she added, not quite truthfully, and smiled charmingly.

A fleeting look of surprise lit those lovely green eyes, then Tara looked rueful. 'I've only been with the firm a few weeks. I moved up from Brisbane to take the position—Hinton, Harcourt & Associates has a fine reputation, even for a smallish town like Cairns.'

'My father would have been delighted to hear you say so,' Nicola said regally, further insulted by the small-town epithet. 'He was the Hinton.'

'So I believe. Brett has told me just how much he admired and respected your father.'

Oh, has he? What else—? Nicola bit off the thought and rose. 'Dinner is ready,' she said graciously, and moved towards the table.

The calamari and Beef Wellington were pronounced excellent, and the conversation was lively. Kim had apparently got over her annoyance—possibly because Tara took the trouble to draw her out and show a keen interest in the charity work she did.

A very skilful operator, Nicola mused once, then grimaced inwardly. Why don't I like her? Well, I know *that*... But did I imagine that she managed to turn a compliment into a subtle put-down, the way she implied that she and Brett had discussed me as if there was a closeness between them that has no right to be there? Or was it simply an accident of words on her part and a touch of paranoia on my part?

But, although they kept it to the minimum, there was no doubt Tara could hold her own—with no 'accident of words'—in the brief discussion of legal matters that was probably inevitable with three lawyers amongst them. She had definite views on the make-up of the High Court, and on the intricacies of Native Title legislation. Definite, concise and intelligent views that caused Rod Mason to view her with admiration again and even Brett to look impressed.

The perfect wife for a lawyer, Nicola found herself thinking involuntarily as Ellen brought in a cheese-board and fruit prior to serving the mocha mousse.

'When do I get to see your work?' Richard Holloway asked at that point, and she turned to him gratefully—anything to distract her from her thoughts...

'Well, those are mine.' She gestured to the candle-sticks. 'And all the pots and urns you may have noticed in the courtyard are, too. But I've got a shed in the garden; I'll take you down after dessert.'

'Can I come as well?' Kim asked a trifle plain-tively.

'With pleasure,' Nicola said warmly. 'You're the one who got me the job—if I'm good enough.'

'Oh, I think we'll all take a look.' Brett glanced at Rod and Tara, who agreed readily.

So they all walked down to the shed in the garden after dessert, and it was Tara who said, 'What a de-lightful hobby, Nicola! I just wish I had time for something like this.'

'Yes, I'm into hobbies,' Nicola shot back, before she could stop herself. 'Keeps me out of mischief, doesn't it, Brett?'

'At times,' he agreed gravely.

'But these are so good!' Kim proclaimed, and looked at Richard for confirmation.

It struck Nicola that Richard, who had been the perfect guest at dinner, had gone into a different mode as he handled a terracotta bowl in the shape of an open clam shell with fluted edges. 'You used a wheel?' he asked with a frown.

'Yes, it wasn't easy.' She shrugged humorously.

'I believe you.' He put the clam shell down and picked up a vase glazed in a swirling riot of peony-pink on misty blue with a gold thread running through it. 'Nor was this, I imagine.'

'Well, I've always admired Moorcroft pottery, and their tube piping technique that gives that raised effect.' She traced a finger down the gold thread. 'Not that I could emulate Moorcroft, but it adds a lovely feel to a piece, don't you think?'

Richard agreed absently and put the vase down carefully. 'Nicola, you and I are in business. Can I come and see you—uh—I've got a meeting with the builders tomorrow—how about the next day, say ten in the morning? I'll bring the plans.'

Nicola blinked, and glanced at Brett.

Who said easily, 'Why not? Congratulations, Mrs Harcourt.' He put his hand briefly over hers without, Nicola suspected, the slightest intimation that his words sounded like death knell to her. 'Shall we go back and have coffee?'

Tara was the last to leave.

She asked Nicola charmingly for a quick tour of the house, and enthused over its design and all that was in it.

'Of course, I didn't do it,' some perverse imp made Nicola say. 'It was Brett's first wife—they were still married when he built the house, so a lot of it is Marietta's taste. Not that you can quarrel with it.'

'You knew her?'

'Very well. She was like an older sister.'

'Does she see much of the children?'

'Whenever she's home Sasha and Chris go to stay with her.'

'I see.' This was said thoughtfully. 'So it was an amicable parting?'

'You'd have to ask Brett that,' Nicola said swiftly. 'And here we are.' They walked back into the lounge and Brett stood up.

'Lovely house, Brett,' Tara said a little hastily, 'and thank you for a lovely evening. Goodness, it's late. I'd better be going!'

But before Brett could answer, Nicola said, 'It was a pleasure to have you, Tara. Wasn't it, darling?' And she slipped her arm through Brett's and laid her head on his shoulder for a moment.

Tara stared at them, and blinked once.

'Yes, it was a pleasure, Tara,' Brett said. 'Uh—I'm sure it's not easy to transplant oneself to a new town.'

Nicola lifted her head and struggled to keep a straight face, because, for once, Brett had sounded less than totally in command.

'Especially a much *smaller* town,' she said gravely. 'I'm sure you'll have a lot of adjustments to make, so if you need any advice, do give me a call. I'm an expert on the best boutiques, hairdressers and so on. And in the meantime,' she added serenely, 'we won't be long out of bed ourselves.' She glanced expressively at Brett and held out her hand to Tara. 'Hope to see you again.'

Tara moved at last.

And Nicola kept her arm linked through Brett's as they walked through the courtyard to the driveway to wave her off.

'Nicola,' Brett said, 'this—'

But she broke in to say quizzically, 'Could you kiss me, Brett? Oh, never mind, I'll do it.' And she stood on tiptoe, wound her arms round his neck and placed her lips on his just as Tara switched on her headlights—and they were bathed in brilliant light.

CHAPTER FOUR

NICOLA chuckled softly as Tara reversed up the drive with a roar, but she didn't remove her arms.

'What do you think you're doing?' Brett enquired dryly.

'Giving as good as I got,' she replied. 'There's only a certain amount of patronage one can take, I'm afraid, and that woman—'

'Are you saying Tara was being patronising? That's ridiculous, Nicola.'

Some of her amusement seeped away. 'Believe me, I'm an expert on the subject. You, for example, patronise me all the time. Just take this very instance. I'm sure you're about to tell me I'm being childish but—' she shrugged, and looked mockingly into his eyes '—it doesn't feel childish. It feels rather nice. How about for you?'

'Nicola,' he said grimly, 'before you get too carried away, why the hell would she be patronising you anyway?'

Nicola opened her eyes at him. 'Don't tell me you don't know—you must be blind. She has you firmly in her sights, Brett. Just imagine the lovely discussions you could have about the High Court, the Supreme Court, the *Family* Court. But I'll tell you one thing—she wouldn't be happy to sit home all day for Sasha and Chris.'

He swore. 'There is *no*—what is this?' And he put his hands up to remove hers.

But she linked her fingers stubbornly and went on. 'As for the lecture you gave me about being discreet the other night, I find it rather ludicrous in light of this. How *dare* you discuss me with her?'

'I haven't—'

'She certainly gave me to understand you had.'

'Nicola, either you're making this all up or you're overtired.'

Something went off inside Nicola's head. 'Not really,' she murmured, 'but I am—since we're in this position—a little curious. It's a long time since I kissed a man. Why don't you help me to brush up my skills, Brett? After all, there are times when you undress me with your eyes—why shouldn't I assess you on a scale of one to ten? It could even add some of the much-needed maturity you so often tell me I lack.'

And she unlocked her fingers, drew them slowly across his shoulders and down the front of his shirt, then she slid her arms around his waist and laid her cheek on his chest. As she did so she felt all his muscles tighten, and she smiled a secret little smile.

Then she felt him relax deliberately, and heard him drawl, 'Don't ever forget you started this, Nicola.'

She hid from him the flash of anger that lit her eyes, and said sweetly, 'Oh, I won't.' And she tilted her face for his kiss.

But although his lips were dry and warm on hers, and his hands moved on her back quite gently, she was tense and stiff, and she made the discovery that to be kissing a man when you were furious with him left you taut with aggression and not sure if you wanted to scratch and bite instead.

He lifted his head. 'I thought this was supposed to be—well, the opposite to making war, Nicola.'

'I hate you, if you must know,' she said through her teeth.

'That's a remarkable about-face, but—' he looked down at her with his lips twisting '—if you didn't go about it like a bull in a china shop—' he held her more firmly as she stiffened in outrage '—these things can be—quite spontaneous.'

'I can't imagine how!'

'Think of it like this, then.' He brought his fingers beneath her hair and massaged the nape of her neck gently. 'There are times when the line of a throat, the curve of a cheek—' he trailed his fingers up her throat and splayed them on her cheek '—the sound of a voice, the arrangement of a figure,' that wandering hand moved downwards with the lightest touch '—the curve of a hip and the sweep of a leg...'

He paused, and his hand moved below the short skirt of her dress, and he smiled slightly as her eyes widened. 'When all of those things can have a powerful effect on a man.'

'I'm sure they can,' she said, but distractedly.

He looked amused. 'And they can make him desire a perfect stranger quite spontaneously. You were going to say?' he asked as she opened her mouth.

But no words came out, because Nicola found herself suddenly mesmerised by this fantasy he'd created, and she could visualise in her mind's eye a scenario that had her, a complete stranger, crossing Brett's path and catching the attention of this tall, clever man just as he'd outlined.

She blinked and swallowed. 'Go...on.'

'And if,' he said slowly, 'I had anything going for you at all, Nicola, the spontaneity might well be mutual. Like this.'

She met this kiss in a completely different frame of mind—oh, where did all that hostility go? she was to wonder later. But it *was* like kissing a stranger, hesitantly at first, drawn uncertainly by the threads of his fantasy but finding it too powerful to resist, then with growing confidence and growing awareness.

An awareness that coursed through her and brought her a sense of wonder, because his body was hard and honed against hers, yet the feel of it was so right and it made her melt against him, slender, soft and quivering with arousal.

But at other times, when they parted to breathe— she at least raggedly—and she saw him watching her narrowly and intently, it made her stare back, and there was a sudden charge of electricity between them, as if she was saying challengingly, I'm not in this alone, am I?

Each time, although only with a gesture, he demonstrated that she wasn't. That was how she discovered that quite ordinary parts of her body became unique with his lips or his fingers on them—the curves of her shoulders, the soft inner sides of her elbows, the hollows at the base of her throat.

And he made her skin feel satin-smooth as he ran his hand down her arm. And she felt both fragile, when he circled her wrist with his fingers and his hand looked big and strong and brown while hers was small and slender, and yet, as he carried her palm to his lips, conscious of a power of her own…

The power to withhold a little, so that he held her closer and tested her ability to remain withdrawn, as he caressed her hips then moved his hands up under her arms and slid them round to cup her breasts. She gave in, but with a little glint of humour in her eyes as she surrendered her mouth to him again.

But in the end he had the ultimate power. After he'd kissed her deeply, and she'd said his name with both wonder and desire, he straightened, held her briefly, and put her away from him.

'What's that supposed to mean?' she murmured breathlessly, and leant against the doorframe for support.

'No more games, Nicola,' he said very quietly.

'Games?' she murmured, and, with a desperate effort not to show her hurt, straightened, touched her mouth, which felt swollen and bruised, and added ruefully, 'I thought we generated quite a bit of emotion as well, but there you go!'

'You did start this,' he reminded her. 'For a variety of reasons, but emotion wasn't mentioned amongst them.'

'So I did! Well, is this what that old saying about playing with matches is all about? Never mind, I've learnt my lesson. I think I'll go to bed—goodnight, Brett.'

He didn't answer, but advanced on her and scooped her up into his arms.

'What are you doing?' she protested.

He carried her over the doorstep.

'Brett! Put me down.' She twisted urgently and

struggled, to no avail. 'Brett, I don't want—don't do this.'

'You don't want to go to bed with me?' he queried. 'Forgive me for saying so, Nicola, but you could have fooled me.'

She stared up into his eyes, and her own were panic-stricken. He watched her for a moment, cynically, then turned into the kitchen and deposited her unceremoniously on the island counter.

'Stay put,' he ordered. 'You've been naughty enough for one night.'

Nicola gasped. 'I...I'm speechless.'

'Good. Try to stay that way.' And he walked through to the dining room.

Nicola looked around. As usual, Ellen had left the kitchen spotless. The slate floors gleamed, the white counter-tops and chrome fittings shone and the yellow chrysanthemum in a pot on the island counter beside her looked bright and cheerful.

Brett came back almost immediately, with two balloon glasses. 'Brandy,' he said. 'You look as if you could do with it.'

She took the glass, stared at its amber contents, then took a solid sip, which caused her to choke as it went down fierily and made her eyes water, but also put some starch back into her soul. She took a smaller sip, then put the glass down beside her—and realised she'd lost one shoe in her undignified struggle and that one of her bra straps had slipped down.

She kicked the remaining shoe off, fished for the errant strap and restored it out of sight, then combed her fingers through her hair. 'Talking of games,' she said then, 'that was a particularly nasty one to play, Brett.'

He raised a wry eyebrow. 'I never had any intention of taking you to bed, Nicola. You were the one who immediately assumed that was the case.'

'Then...why...?' She stared at him confusedly.

'All I was ever going to do was this—' he inclined his head towards the counter '—so that we could talk this out rather than have you scuttling off to bed all mortified and—whatever. By the same token, many men—' a grim little glint beamed her way '—would not have been so obliging, Nicola.'

'I know *that*, but you're not "many men",' she protested, and immediately bit her lip and eyed him warily.

But he only smiled slightly—a cool twisting of his lips. 'Then let's move on. Would you care to explain why you were so determined to have me kiss you, against my better judgement?'

Nicola flinched, and put a hand to her mouth involuntarily. 'If that was against your better judgement I'd hate to see what you could do in accord with it— uh...' She saw the fleeting look of amusement in his eyes, but it was gone in an instant and her shoulders slumped. 'I—you may not believe me—but tonight I was made to feel...'

She stopped, then said with more spirit, 'You were there, Brett! *"What a delightful hobby, Nicola!"'* she mimicked. 'And—*"I just wish I had time for something like this."* She...' She paused, and frowned. 'I'm not getting through to you, am I?'

He shrugged. 'It seems an excessive length to go to because you'd been made to feel somewhat inadequate, and she probably had no idea she was being patronising. But what about this desire to brush up certain skills that you mentioned?' he said with irony.

Nicola breathed frustratedly. He was leaning back with his broad shoulders propped against the door-frame, his arms folded across his chest, and there was absolutely no evidence that anything momentous had happened to him. She hadn't even left any lipstick on him, because it had all worn off earlier.

'It was one of those foolish things you say in the heat of the moment.' She said it quietly, but her gaze was level, even a touch severe.

He grimaced, but said, 'So it wasn't a prelude to getting to know Richard Holloway better?'

'When—*if* I ever decide to get to know him in that way, it'll be entirely between him and me, Brett. So don't say another word about Richard Holloway!'

'Bravo,' he murmured, but with a trace of unmistakable satire. And he added wryly, at her scorching look, 'You're pretty free with your comments on what you perceive my choices in that line might be, but I shall desist.'

She compressed her lips and slid off the counter abruptly. 'I am going to bed now, and I should warn you that any attempt to trick me or lecture me on the error of my ways is liable to make me bite and scratch and kick! If you think you're as pure as the driven snow—'

She stopped as he detained her with a hand on her wrist, and her blue eyes blazed, but he said, 'I'm not going to do any of those things—and neither are you.' He waited, and watched all the expressions chase through her eyes, but did not release her. It was like being up against an iron will she had no answer for.

She swallowed. 'So?'

'So? As a matter of fact, I apologise—for not being as pure as the driven snow—but what you don't seem to realise is that there are times when men…can't help being men.

'And—' he overrode her as she opened her mouth '—I also apologise for the fact that you were made to feel uncomfortable this evening. Although—' he looked fleetingly amused '—I doubt she'll make that mistake again.' He drew her loosely into his arms. 'What a night, one way or the other,' he murmured. 'I thought at one stage that Kim was going to assassinate Rod.'

Nicola tried to resist it, but she couldn't. Her lips curved into a reluctant smile, then she was laughing helplessly. 'You're right. If looks could kill—'

'We'd have been having to appoint a new District Court Judge.'

They laughed together, and it was warm, and she felt some of the tension drain out of her as he hugged her gently and kissed the top of her head. Then she felt him stiffen, and realised he'd raised his head. She turned in his arms to see Chris standing in the doorway, staring at them.

'What is it, Chris?' she said.

'I was having a nightmare about horrible big snakes and I was thirsty.' He waved a red plastic mug, then rushed on excitedly. 'So you *are* a real mum, Nicky, and Sasha was wrong. Oh, boy, wait until I tell her this—she thinks she's so clever—can I hug, too?'

'Of course you can,' Brett said, and Chris raced

over to them and flung his arms around their legs. Brett released Nicola unhurriedly and picked him up. 'Back to bed, young man. Here, I'll fill your mug for you.'

'But what if the snakes are under my bed?' Chris objected.

'I'll have a look,' Brett said, and carried him out.

Nicola unfroze, but was still leaning on the counter with her face in her hands when Brett returned.

'How is he?' she asked fearfully.

'Quite reassured. He'll be asleep in no time. Nicola—'

'Brett, what are we going to do?' she broke in agitatedly. 'He said—'

'I heard what he said, but this is not the time to try to sort it out. Go to bed, Nicola—goodnight,' he said quietly, but quite definitely.

Her bedroom had apple-green walls, a double brass bedstead with a hand appliquéd white quilt, white furniture, a beautiful Chinese rug in pinks and greens and a ruby velvet-covered couch set against the foot of the bed.

The couch was a favourite spot of Nicola's when she wanted to think, and it also brought into full view one of her favourite possessions. She had a shower, changed into pink and white polka dot pyjamas and lay down on it, swept her hair over the armrest and stared at the picture on the opposite wall.

It was a framed poster actually from The Cloisters, the branch of the New York Metropolitan Museum devoted to art of the Middle Ages. In wool tapestry, of Franco-Flemish origin from the early sixteenth century, it depicted a unicorn in captivity. As a child she'd woven magic stories about how it had been captured and how it could be released.

She knew it off by heart—the small wooden corral, the droplets of blood on the unicorn's creamy hide as it lay penned, the ornate collar round its neck and the chain to the fence, the dense, flowery meadow surrounding it—and it struck her suddenly that there were some similarities between her position and the unicorn's.

Well, she mused, no blood, but bruised and battered in the region of the heart would be a good way to explain how I feel at the moment.

I can't believe Tara Wells would have acted entirely on her own; he must have shown some interest in her. They did have dinner the other night, for example. And why else would he suddenly discuss Marietta with me this evening, as he's never done before? Was he afraid I'd make a scene on Marietta's behalf—not knowing what it would do to *me*?

She turned on her side, slipped her hands beneath her cheek and remembered being in his arms, the sheer heaven of it—but now, irrevocably, tainted by the aftermath.

Tears welled and she dashed at them impatiently. The most lowering thought of all, she discovered, was that by her own hand she'd forced Brett into a 'men will be men' situation. She didn't want to think of him like that, she found, and least of all did she want him to think of her as capable of those kind of games.

It was the hardest thing she'd ever done, to face Brett over the breakfast table the next morning, but he, at least, appeared entirely unconcerned by the events of the night before.

It was a sparkling morning again, and the sea, beyond the louvres of the family room where they ate informally, was a pale blue reflection of the sky.

'How did you sleep?' he asked.

She buttered some toast for Sasha. 'Not too badly. How about you?'

'OK. What's on today?'

'The usual.'

'No flying lessons?'

She grimaced, and thought how pleasant it would be to soar above the clouds—not that there were any today—and forget all the complications of her life below them. 'My instructor is on holiday.'

'I see.' He poured himself some coffee. 'I thought we might have a barbecue on the beach this evening.'

Sasha and Chris snapped to attention and chorused, 'Yes, please!'

But Nicola eyed their father suspiciously.

He said to the children, 'I'll drop you off at school this morning, which means you've got fifteen minutes precisely to be ready. Off you go.'

They scampered off.

'As you said to me last night, Nicola—' he eyed her lazily '—what's that supposed to mean? The way you're looking at me,' he added satirically, in case she was tempted to feign misunderstanding.

She held onto her temper and shrugged. 'That I'm not a five or six-year-old who can be placated by a barbecue on the beach, probably. Excuse me,' she added and put her napkin on the table. 'I'll help them to get ready.'

'Stay where you are, Nicola,' he said quietly, but with a wealth of command in his steady hazel gaze. 'It's about time they learnt to do a few things for themselves.'

'I—are you criticising—' She broke off and stared at him angrily.

He smiled dryly. 'As a matter of fact, I'm not criticising your management of them—rather, your desire to scuttle away from me. Because it means you're still in a state of high dudgeon over what happened last night.'

She looked around the bright, comfortable family room, with its rattan furniture, and picked up her napkin to clench her fingers round it. 'Strangely enough, I am. Further reflection, you see, on top of the way you're acting—like some absolute autocrat—'

'Nicola, let's not get dramatic. It's a bit early in the day for it,' he murmured prosaically. 'I merely thought, for their sakes, a barbecue on the beach—which is a special treat they love, and you usually love too,' he said significantly, 'might restore some tranquillity to the household. For all of us, but *them* most of all.'

'They don't know—they...' She stopped frustratedly.

'They're geniuses at picking up any kind of vibes flying around, wouldn't you agree?'

Nicola eyed him. He was wearing a cream shirt and a lightweight fawn suit, the jacket of which was hung over the back of his chair. His tie was a cinnamon-brown with narrow diagonal cream and red stripes. Both the tie and the shirt had been a Christmas present from her, but it gave her no pleasure at the moment to see him wearing them.

Nor did it please her much to think that this crisp, shaved man of the world, with his thick brown hair tidy and gleaming, and all that barely concealed sharpness of mind, all that barely subdued aura of power that affected women so dynamically, was about to set forth *into* the world.

While I stay at home like a good little wife—is that it? she wondered. Or is it the thought of Tara Wells out there, being all professional and equally intelligent, although at the same time no doubt beautifully presented? She glanced down at herself ruefully. She'd woken late and thrown on a pink T-shirt with denim shorts and hurriedly tied her hair back in a ponytail. She felt, she found, far from sharp of mind and unusually power*less*.

But she straightened her spine. 'Whatever you say, bwana!'

'Been catching up on your Wilbur Smith, Nicola?' he asked lazily.

'Now there's a thought,' she retaliated. 'Scrub Tibet—I've always wanted to go to Africa.'

'I would scrub Africa too, if I were you at the moment,' he drawled. 'Why don't you stick to one thing at a time? Pottery, for example? Having made such a hit there,' he added gently, but nonetheless lethally.

Her smile, which was more a baring of her teeth, caused him to laugh softly, and he stood up and hooked his jacket off the chair. 'My, my, we are having a rather mindless domestic, aren't we, Nicola?'

She watched him shrug into it and was amazed to feel a tremor run through her, because if the attraction of his body had been a torment to her over the last two years, the events of last night had heightened it unbelievably.

She could feel, suddenly, through her pores, the imprint of his hard strength on her slightness. She remembered, as if she could still feel him through the palms of her hands, the lean lines of his back and the powerful muscles of his shoulders, his taut diaphragm. But most all she could feel in herself how it had all stirred her senses, her own body.

But the unbelievable part of it was, as she clenched her teeth and her hands, that she could be so angry with him and yet still be so affected by him.

She could have kissed Sasha and Chris for arriving at the table, breathless and laughing, their clothing somewhat askew, full of assurances that they were ready!

'Here, I'll just…straighten you up a bit.' And she went about it without looking at Brett once.

But she couldn't evade his gaze when it was done.

'See you tonight, then,' he said.

'All right,' she replied, and started to stack plates.

But he pointedly didn't move.

Her hands hovered, then she straightened and said impatiently, 'What now?'

Their gazes clashed. 'Are you all right?' he asked quietly.

No, I'm not! What do you expect? But she didn't say it. She shrugged, and forced herself to smile. 'Fine. Hold thumbs it doesn't rain!'

'That almost sounds as if you're praying for it,' he said, and walked out.

*   *   *

It didn't rain. It was a clear, beautiful afternoon as she packed the picnic basket.

'Can we swim?' Sasha asked.

'I should think so. They've taken the stinger net in. Put your togs on under your clothes, but we'd better take jumpers for later.'

Brett arrived home at five-thirty and they drove down to Yorkeys Knob beach, a long stretch of sand facing Cape Grafton with a park behind it. They chose a spot and the children and Brett started scouting for firewood before it got dark. Then they all had a swim, Nicola in a one-piece sapphire-blue costume with white flowers on it.

'Brrr...' She ran up the beach, leaving Brett and the children frolicking, dried herself, threw on a track-suit top and lit the fire.

She'd brought a portable grid and long forks, and simple fare. Sausages and bread, some sandwiches to keep the hunger pangs at bay while the sausages cooked, and homemade toffee apples for dessert. She'd also brought a flask of coffee, and juice for the children, but she discovered a chilled bottle of wine in a slide-on thermo-pack, and two glasses that she hadn't put into the picnic hamper.

She was staring down at the bottle in her hands when Brett and the children ran up.

'Why not?' he said lightly as she looked up at him. 'I even remembered a corkscrew.' He took the bottle from her.

She didn't have to answer. Sasha and Chris were turning blue with cold and shivering exaggeratedly, showering droplets of water everywhere. She jumped

up and began to towel them vigorously, then made
them change into dry clothes and sit by the fire.

When they were warm again it was almost dark,
and they started racing up and down the beach, playing leapfrog then hopscotch.

'Such energy,' Brett murmured ruefully as he ar-
ranged the sausages on the grid. 'Here.' He handed
her a glass of wine.

He'd pulled on an old football jersey over his costume, and with his damp hair hanging in his eyes he
couldn't have looked less like the super-executive of
the morning. But nonetheless attractive, she thought
with a pang. And why do I get the feeling I'm about
to be exposed to that rare charm no one can exert like
Brett?

She was right, she discovered. He went out of his
way to make the barbecue a success. He insisted she
relax on the tartan rug while he took care of the cook-
ing, and dished up hot sausages on pieces of bread
with tomato sauce for the children and a mixture of
tomato sauce and mustard for themselves. He managed to calm Sasha and Chris down so they could eat
properly by playing 'I Spy' with them. Then he pro-
duced two torches, so they could wander around and
explore after they'd finished eating.

And he involved Nicola in it all, although he
wouldn't let her move.

'How was that?' he asked finally, stretched out on
the blanket with his head propped on his hand, having
built up the fire again and replenished their glasses.

Nicola hugged her knees. The woodsmoke was ar-
omatic, drifting against the darkened sky in wreaths
of pale grey. The glow of the fire was not only warm-

ing but comforting, and the tide was lapping against the beach. There was a pale, prim little new moon rising over the ocean, and the two bobbing circles of torchlight made sure they knew where Sasha and Chris were.

'It was very nice. Thank you.'

He sat up. 'Do I detect a slight reservation in your voice?'

She picked up her glass and sipped some wine. 'If you really want to know, I couldn't think of anything I'd rather be doing—under normal circumstances. But…' She shrugged. 'Oh, well, it doesn't matter.'

'Tell me.'

The firelight was bronzing his hair and the skin of his long bare legs, and she was gripped suddenly by a fantasy of her own. That they could be on a deserted beach anywhere in the world, just the two of them. Perhaps—thinking of Africa—even with wild animals prowling around, kept at bay by the fire.

How marvellous it would be to crawl into a tent with him. To strip her top and her costume off by the light of a lantern and to see his hands on her bare skin, darker and lean and strong as they slid around the ivory skin of her breasts to the pale rose of her nipples…

'Nicola?'

She swallowed and looked up at last, hoping desperately that the warmth of the fire would account for the colour she felt prickling the surface of her cheeks. She cradled her glass in her hands and wished she could apply the chill to her face. 'I…perhaps I don't bounce back from encounters like last night quite as readily as you do, Brett. That's all.'

'I thought we'd laid it to rest.'

'All the same I felt…I felt a bit cheap,' she confessed.

He raised an eyebrow at her. 'This morning I could have sworn you were fighting mad.'

She tossed her hair back. 'I was, but that was because you provoked me.'

'And—just now?' he queried idly, but with a faint frown in his eyes.

'What do you mean?' But her heart had started to beat uncomfortably.

'You were deep in thought and then thoroughly embarrassed.'

Damn you, Brett Harcourt, she thought, and she only just stopped herself from asking him how he could tell. 'It…' She paused. 'Well, if you can concoct fantasies, so can I. Indeed—' she looked at him with a spark of irony '—if you hadn't done so in the first place, I—well…' She drained her glass, put it down and jumped up restlessly to start to pack up the picnic basket.

He stayed where he was. 'About us? And this beach?'

She didn't answer, but started to shake out towels.

'Do you know what would happen tonight if we were properly married?' He studied her meditatively. 'I mean—and here's something for you to think about, Nicola—we'd go to bed together.' He paused, and his gaze lingered on her bare legs, then lifted to meet her eyes. 'And because of the romantic elements of a night like tonight, most husbands would not be able to keep their hands off you.'

'Why—should I think about that?'

'I'm not sure if you realise,' he said slowly, 'that once you allow a man the freedom of your body, you can't always call all the shots.'

She stared down at him wide-eyed as his clever hazel gaze roamed up and down her again, leisurely, almost as if he were imagining having the freedom of her body, and it sent the blood surging through her veins once more.

'Nothing to say to that, Nicola?' he queried.

She threw the towel down and put her hands on her hips. 'Brett, don't...' Her shoulders slumped suddenly. 'This is *difficult*. Don't—make anything of it.'

Their gazes caught and held—his intent, hers reflecting a helplessness she couldn't hide.

He stood up at last, and took her hand. She tried to pull it away but he wouldn't let her. 'It's all right. I'm not going to make anything of it, but I never thought you were cheap—and there's nothing wrong with the odd fantasy.' He looked wry. 'So long as you realise that's what it is.'

Surprise made her breath catch in her throat.

'And you're right,' he added, not quite smiling. 'A fire and a beach, a new moon—all dangerously fitting for fantasies. But here comes reality.' He dropped her hand and put his arm around her shoulders—as Sasha and Chris raced up.

'See! What did I tell you?' Chris asked Sasha. 'They do hug.'

And Sasha heaved a sigh that spoke volumes. 'Now we know you're not going to leave us, Nicky! We were quite worried about it, weren't we, Chris? Because we thought you weren't real,' she added, by way of explanation. 'A real mum.'

* * *

Nicola was too confused and too tired to do anything but tumble into bed when they got home. She'd seen Brett watching her once, while she'd put Sasha and Chris to bed, narrowly and probingly, but she'd simply shaken her head.

His hazel gaze had lingered on the shadows beneath her eyes and the strain evident around her mouth, but he'd gone away to his study after wishing them all goodnight.

Sleep had come at once, but all night long it had been threaded with dreams of beaches and lions roaring around camp fires and herself, searching for Brett but unable to find him. She woke late the next morning, feeling about as refreshed as if she had been on an all-night safari.

It wasn't until after she was dressed that she noticed a message from Brett on her dressing table. All it said was that he had to be in court this morning but he'd see her tonight.

She screwed the paper up, not sure if she wanted to laugh or scream with frustration, and tossed it into the wastepaper basket with a definite groan of something—causing Ellen, who happened to be passing her open doorway, to stop abruptly.

'You OK?'

'Fine,' she lied. 'Well, it was quite a night, one way or another.'

'So Brett mentioned. He said to let you sleep in. He dropped Sasha to school and Chris to kindy. Was it them?'

Nicola blinked. 'No! No, they were as good as gold. They loved the barbecue; they always do. Heavens, I had no idea it was so late.'

Ellen eyed her. 'You don't look too bright, I must say. Sure you're not sickening for something?'

'No.' Nicola laughed and sniffed the air. 'Just wait and see what a cup of your coffee does for me—oh, by the way—' she suddenly remembered Richard Holloway, but not with the enthusiasm she feigned for Ellen's benefit '—I forgot to tell you, but I've got a pottery commission!'

Richard arrived on the dot of ten o'clock.

Nicola took him into the den and he spread out his folder of designs on the maple desk. 'Reef and rainforest is the theme,' he explained again. 'Which is why your clam shells would fit in so well. I was really impressed with them. Well, to be honest I was even more impressed with your glazes, but...' He shrugged.

'Have you ever seen clams in their natural state?' Nicola said slowly. 'I mean, alive as opposed to being doorstops and ashtrays?'

He shook his head.

'They're quite amazing. They're embedded in the reef, and all you see is this wavy line, but as they open these dark, fleshy lips appear, striped and spotted in the most fantastic colours—emerald, magenta, gold—and when they're startled, they shoot up a jet of water.'

Richard stared at her. 'A clam fountain—what a brilliant idea. Could you get the glazes right?'

'I don't see why not. And—this is just a thought; I've been dying to try my hand at one—have you ever seen an apple sea cucumber?'

He shook his head again, and she walked over to

the bookcase. 'There's a picture here somewhere...'
Her hand hovered, then she pulled a book out and
they pored over it. 'They're so colourful it's hard to
believe they're real.'

'And you could do this?'

'I'm sure I could.'

He started to sketch rapidly on a piece of cartridge
paper, and a delightful clam fountain and sea cucumber garden took shape amidst coral and tropical fish.

'That's lovely,' Nicola said, genuinely entranced.
'Of course I don't know anything about plumbing—'

'That'll be my headache.' He grimaced. 'But it's
entirely possible.'

'I can just imagine people—particularly kids—
watching it for ages, waiting for the clams to spout.'

'Particularly *little* kids,' he said significantly, 'who
beg their mums to take them to see it again and again,
and, of course, once they're in the centre—well, that's
half the battle. But if we do this properly, it won't
only be the kids.'

She laughed. 'Crass marketing techniques,
Richard?'

He agreed ruefully. 'But there'll be a plaque with
your name on it, and I'm positive more commissions
would flow on from it. Which leads us on to the business angle.'

They discussed that, then he hesitated and said,
'Brett—doesn't object to you doing this, Nicola?'

'No. Well, you heard him on Tuesday night, didn't
you?'

'But before Tuesday night I got the impression he
wasn't that keen. Or at all keen, to be more accurate.'

Nicola chewed her lip in embarrassment. 'Uh, perhaps not...I suppose you're wondering—' She stopped awkwardly.

'Whether Sasha got it wrong?' he said gently.

'Richard, I can't...look, he knows now how much I want to do this, so it's OK, I promise.'

He sat back. 'Then could I just say this, Nicola? I'd very much like to be a friend as well as a business associate.'

'Why not?' she murmured, but looked away after one swift glance told her there was more than friendship in his nice grey eyes.

He left not long afterwards, but asked if he could come back the following evening with a proper drawing and specifications.

Nicola picked Chris up from kindy and they had lunch with Ellen in the kitchen, but she was restless and jumpy. Then she made an abrupt decision.

'Ellen, could you hold the fort this afternoon? I need to go into town.'

'Will do,' Ellen said obligingly. 'I might take them to the park after I pick Sasha up from school.'

'Yowee!' Chris said enthusiastically.

Nicola decided to change, and chose what to wear with care. But what if Brett is out of the office? she asked herself as she stared at her clothes, and answered herself—I can't sit around doing nothing; that's all there is to it.

She finally settled on an ice-blue crêpe trouser suit. The jacket was long-line and double-breasted, with short sleeves, and she slipped on white court shoes with square toes and silver Cuban heels and slung a white quilted leather purse with a silver chain over her shoulder. Dressy enough to be seen in the offices of Hinton, Harcourt & Associates, she decided, and dressy enough for the wife of the senior partner—not to mention dressy enough for Tara Wells.

She drove her silver hatchback down the Knob and through the village at the prescribed mileage, then speeded up as the houses gave way to cane fields.

Along the highway there was more evidence that Cairns was a sugar town, as cane trains laden with cut stalks shuttled along.

But once she'd left the northern beach suburbs behind, and passed the airport, it became obvious that Cairns was also a tourist destination. Many motels lined the main roads and the tourists, lured from all over the world to the wonders of the Great Barrier Reef and the world heritage-listed Daintry Rainforest, were easily detectable in their bright holiday clothing and with their cameras at the ready.

It wasn't these things that occupied her mind, though, as she parked her car in Sheridan Street and sat in it for several minutes. It was what she was going to say to Brett that caused her palms to be damp and her brow to be furrowed with indecision. Had the time come for the simple truth? she wondered painfully.

The reception area of Hinton, Harcourt & Associates was impressive. Mottled marble floors, mirrored walls, exotic potted palms, and behind the reception desk a familiar face.

'Why, Nicola,' Fiona Grant, who had once been her father's secretary, said delightedly. 'This is a lovely surprise. How are you?'

NO RISK, NO OBLIGATION TO BUY...NOW OR EVER!

GUARANTEED

PLAY "ROLL A DOUBLE" AND YOU GET FREE GIFTS! HERE'S HOW TO PLAY:

1. Peel off label from front cover. Place it in space provided at right. With a coin, carefully scratch off the silver dice. Then check the claim chart to see what we have for you – TWO FREE BOOKS and a mystery gift – ALL YOURS! ALL FREE!

2. Send back this card and you'll receive brand-new Harlequin Presents® novels. These books have a cover price of $3.75 each in the U.S. and $4.25 each in Canada, but they are yours to keep absolutely free.

3. There's no catch. You're under no obligation to buy anything. We charge nothing – ZERO – for your first shipment. And you don't have to make any minimum number of purchases – not even one!

4. The fact is, thousands of readers enjoy receiving books by mail from the Harlequin Reader Service®. They like the convenience of home delivery...they like getting the best new novels BEFORE they're available in stores...and they love our discount prices!

5. We hope that after receiving your free books you'll want to remain a subscriber. But the choice is yours – to continue or cancel any time at all! So why not take us up on our invitation, with no risk of any kind. You'll be glad you did!

'Fine, thanks, Fiona! How are you?'

It took all of ten minutes to be told, and to comment interestedly on the state of Fiona's health, wealth and otherwise, but then that good lady frowned and said, 'Brett didn't mention you were coming in, Nicola.'

'He didn't know. But he's here, isn't he?'

'Y-e-s,' Fiona said cautiously, 'but he's in a staff meeting and—'

'Then I'll just pop up. It's rather important, Fiona. Don't worry,' she added humorously, 'I'll take the blame.' And she trod up the marble staircase.

There was no one in the outer office, where his secretary should have been, so Nicola shrugged, walked to the door of the inner sanctum, tapped on it and opened it without waiting for a response.

There were only two people at the alleged staff meeting, she discovered, as Brett looked up from the other side of the vast oak desk that had once been her father's.

The desk was littered with files and documents, and there was no doubting her husband was annoyed at this untimely interruption. His expression was distinctly irritated and impatient as he swung the silver pen between his fingers, then threw it down with a clunk.

The second person at the meeting was on the same side of the desk as he was, leaning over his shoulder to scan a document, and she wore a pewter silk blouse with a jungle-green denim skirt. Her dark hair was luxuriously and wonderfully styled, as if she'd just walked out of a hairdresser's, and the faintest trace of Chanel No 5 lingered on the air—Tara Wells.

CHAPTER FIVE

'NICOLA—what are you doing here?'

It occurred to Brett as soon as he'd spoken that he'd been less than diplomatic as his wife bent her lovely but severe gaze upon him. It also occurred to him that this beautifully groomed and imperious Nicola bore little resemblance to the tousled although no less lovely creature of two nights ago and the night before...

How the hell I am going to defuse this? he wondered somewhat grimly. I must have been mad.

Nicola switched her gaze from him to Tara, and said, 'Sorry to break this up, Tara, but I need to speak to Brett.'

Tara blinked, then pinned a smile on. 'Thank you for a lovely evening the other night. I was going to ring you! How did you get on with Richard this morning, by the way? It was this morning he was coming, wasn't it?'

'Fine,' Nicola said brightly, but made no attempt to elaborate.

'Well...' Tara gathered the files together. 'I'll leave you two together.' But when she was halfway to the door she turned and said, 'Perhaps you and Brett would come and have dinner with me some time? My unit is nearly finished—I had it redecorated; it's much more *me* now.'

'Thank you very much,' Nicola said formally.

Tara hesitated, then left with barely concealed reluctance.

'Not spying on me by any chance, Nicola?' Brett drawled, lying back in his chair.

'What makes you think that?' she shot back.

'Your unheralded arrival, and your look of deep suspicion when you saw who was here.'

'I only arrived unheralded because I was afraid you'd find some way of fobbing me off, Brett,' Nicola said evenly. 'As for how I may have looked, I'm quite sure Tara could have conducted any business with you from *this* side of the desk. I also wouldn't have thought that could be classified as a ''staff meeting'', but you live and learn.' She unhooked her purse from her shoulder and put it down on the desk with a rattle of the chain.

'You're being ridiculous, Nicola.'

'Am I? We'll see. But that's not why I came. What are we going to do, Brett?'

He sat up. 'Couldn't this have waited until tonight?'

'No, it could not! I'm going out of my mind worrying about it.'

He studied her for a moment, then reached for the phone and instructed his secretary to hold all calls and interruptions and to bring in coffee.

'*Thank* you.' Nicola sat down.

He grimaced. 'Do you have any suggestions?'

'No. I've gone over it again and again—' she rubbed her brow and sighed '—but I keep coming back to square one. I thought at one stage that the sooner I went the better, but now it looks as if it's too late. I can't seem to think straight,' she added unhappily.

'How *did* it go with Richard this morning?'

She shot him an old-fashioned look.

'Just humour me, Nicola,' he murmured.

'Fine! I've got a commission to make some clams and some apple sea cucumbers and they're going to build them into a fountain.'

'What about the practical side of things? Deadlines, contracts and so on?'

She gripped her hands in her lap, then forced herself to relax. 'I've six months. The centre doesn't open for another nine. I'm to be paid an exorbitant fee.' She shrugged. 'Well, it may be the going rate for all I know, there's going to be a little plaque with my name on it, and I have a contract to sign.'

'Good,' he said. 'I'll go over it for you.'

'One of the advantages of having a lawyer in the family,' she said dryly, as his secretary, a fearsome bottle blonde and normally a formidable lady, knocked and opened the door, bearing a tray.

But she paused on the threshold and looked surprised as she saw Nicola. 'Oh! Mrs Harcourt! I didn't see you arrive, I'm sorry.' She looked around the room, as if to make sure there was no one else lurking about. 'I'd already gone to make the coffee.' She came into the room and put the tray on the desk.

Nicola studied the two cups and lifted a briefly sardonic gaze to her husband. But she said warmly to his secretary, 'How are you, Margaret? I haven't seen you for ages.'

'Really well, thank you, and you do look lovely today, Mrs Harcourt. Uh...' she pointed to a little silver dish '...I brought some of my home-made macaroons in for Mr Harcourt this morning. Hope you enjoy them.'

Nicola maintained a straight face as she thanked Margaret, but once the door closed on her she turned to Brett and said humorously, 'You do get them in— at all ages and in all shapes. I suppose it is a bit of a problem.'

He didn't respond as she stood up to pour the coffee.

'Do *you* have any solutions?' she asked with some irony as she sat down again.

He picked up the silver pen and doodled on a yellow legal pad for a moment, then raised his gaze to hers. 'It could all be a storm in a teacup, Nicola.'

She blinked. 'That your children now think we are man and wife—in every sense of the words—and that they were *worried* about me leaving? You surprise me, Brett.'

He lifted his shoulders. 'Let's not get too emotional, Nicola. They are only five and six. I wouldn't be at all surprised if, assuming we carry on as before, they settle down and we do so too.'

She gazed at him, all set to refute this, but common sense asserted itself. 'They may,' she said slowly at last, 'but surely it's only prolonging things? They're still going to wonder as they get older, and—'

'They're also going to become less dependent on you as they get older, and better able to understand things.'

'But…' She frowned with an effort to think straight again. 'Where does that leave me?'

He got up and came round to sit on the corner of the desk. 'You have a few options,' he said quietly.

'Staying with us until you're twenty-three is probably the most sensible of them.'

Her eyes widened. 'I couldn't.'

'Why not?' he asked conversationally.

'I...' She stared at him helplessly.

'So far as your rising career as a potter goes, you couldn't be better set up than you are now, and if it is a career you're hankering for—' he smiled briefly '—now you've got it, you might find all the angst, inadequacy and uncertainty you've been experiencing is gone.'

If she could have found the words to refute this without giving herself away she would have done so, but there was worse to come, she discovered.

'Another option,' he went on, 'is to do with what happened two nights ago.'

She swallowed. 'I don't...' She cleared her throat. 'I don't think we should place much importance on what happened two nights ago.'

'No?' There was a gleam of pure mockery in his eyes for a moment, then he went on gravely, 'Why is that?'

'I told you...what happened.'

'You told me a lot of things, gave me a lot of possible motivations, but I can't help wondering whether it wasn't quite simple, actually. Simple jealousy. Of Tara.'

Nicola stood up and her hand flashed out, but he caught her wrist. 'My, my, you are becoming a little wildcat, Nicola,' he said gently, but lethally.

'I'm not—you're enough to make me...do anything,' she retorted bitterly. 'Let me go.'

'No. Not until I'm assured you don't have any further violent intentions towards me. Unless...' He narrowed his eyes and looked her up and down, taking in the way her breathing was affecting the front of her ice-blue jacket, then his gaze returned to hers. 'Unless this is something else?'

'What?'

'Another manifestation of your sudden desire to experiment? Test your powers of attraction, that kind of thing,' he suggested.

'Now why would I bother?' she countered swiftly. 'You made it so very clear that I was only to be taught a lesson. You could hardly,' she said with irony, 'expect me to believe there was any attraction on your side, and—'

'That's debatable,' he broke in.

'And...' She paused with a frown. 'What do you mean?'

'You must have a short memory,' he murmured, and his gaze roamed over her in a way that brought a tide of colour to her cheeks.

To make matters worse, she was again afflicted by the consciousness that this tall, clever man, even when she thought she hated him, as now, could reduce her body to an incredible desire to be one with his. Even now, she thought with some despair, I still want him.

She took a breath and said barely audibly, 'Let me go, Brett.'

He released her wrist but made no other move, and she shook out her hair and ran her fingers through it. He watched enigmatically, and she sat down again and said tensely, 'Where were we?'

The faintest smile touched his mouth. 'Examining

the possibility of you being jealous of Tara. Nicola, about what happened two nights ago—'

'Look, you got me in very cleverly with a—fantasy you conjured up, but that's all it was. I'm sure it meant no more to *you* than that.'

'Well...' he raised a wry eyebrow '...since you mention it, that's what I thought this might be. Another fantasy—let's say *yet* another fantasy.'

Her cheeks burned, but her eyes burned brighter— with anger. 'That's not fair, Brett.'

'No? All the same, this time is a more exciting, rather dangerous encounter. Didn't you know that to be thoroughly angry with each other can lend an extra dimension to sensual encounters? Or, to put it more bluntly, that slapping a man's face can be an invitation of another kind?' he said softly.

Nicola choked. Then she managed to say, 'It's not that. As for Tara, she does...yes—' she gestured frustratedly '—she annoys me intensely. For example, what business is it of hers how I got on with Richard?'

Brett smiled faintly. 'She's probably got that message by now, too. But, to get back to the options I mentioned, there is another one. We could...' He paused, and their gazes clashed as Nicola had a premonition of something momentous to come. 'We could make this a real and very proper marriage.'

Her lips parted and her voice seemed not to want to work, until finally she said huskily, 'Would you really do that, Brett? Marry—completely—someone you don't love, for the sake of your children?'

His lips twisted. 'Love...is not as simple as you may think, Nicola.'

She stared into his hazel eyes. 'Is that a way of saying once bitten twice shy?'

A nerve flickered in his jaw and he hesitated, then answered, 'Perhaps. But we have an awful lot going for us. We live in a lot more domestic harmony than many others—the Masons, for example.' He looked wry. 'We don't drive each other crazy with any irritating little habits—I'm sure they'd have surfaced by now. And we cope pretty well with two children. Believe me, that's quite a test. You could almost say we were very properly married in most respects.'

Nicola looked away and remembered wondering whether to tell Brett the truth this afternoon... But, if anything, this catalogue of what they had going for them said it all, she thought. He didn't love her, perhaps he would never love again, but at least he'd been honest.

I could still do it, though, she thought. It would take away all this awful pretence. But what else would it achieve? Perhaps it's what I should have done straight away, instead of getting angry and—all the rest. But—no, then he'd feel sorry for me...

'And,' he said, 'what happened the other night, and last night—talking of fantasies and moons et cetera— is an indication that that side of marriage would be no problem.'

She flinched inwardly and looked back at him, a clear, blue, but thoroughly unreadable look.

'Nicola,' he said, but she got up abruptly and walked over to the window with her arms wrapped around her, as if to ward off the chill that was invading her.

'Nicola,' he said again, from right behind her, although she hadn't heard him cross the carpet, 'tell me what you're thinking. Something has changed and I need to know.'

It was nearly a full minute before she turned. 'All right. Tara—in a way she did change things. I suppose she highlighted the fact that I haven't made anything of my life so far—'

'Tara is over thirty, Nicola. And having a law degree, or being a concert pianist for that matter, is only one area of a life. I've told you before, you're intelligent and artistic, and there's no need to feel inadequate.'

She raised her eyebrows. 'It wasn't only that. I...well, I have to confess I suddenly looked around and pictured her in charge of the house, of the children. I could see her lording it over Ellen and—I discovered I didn't like the thought of it one bit.'

'So that means,' he said quietly, 'you enjoy being mistress of my house, Nicola?'

'I...I must,' she said shakily. 'Not that it's so surprising,' she added with an attempt at humour. 'Most girls would give their eye-teeth to be in my position. You're a very marriageable man in most respects, Brett.'

He didn't reply immediately, although a spark of amusement lit his eyes—only to die almost at once.

'And then there is the fact,' she went on, while she still had the courage, 'that to be part of a family means such a lot to me. More than most, I guess. But I still—I mean, it can't go on for ever, so...' She shrugged.

'There's no reason it can't go on for the time being,

as it has been going on, but—' He stopped and swore as the phone rang.

He strode across the room and picked it up. 'Margaret, I thought I told you—' He stopped and his expression of irritation altered to something different. Nicola took an unsteady breath.

'What is it?' she said fearfully as he put down the phone after a few curt enquiries.

'Chris. He fell off the jungle gym in the park and broke his leg. Ellen called an ambulance and they've just arrived at the Calvary Hospital.'

'Oh, no!' Nicola went white. 'Why did I leave them!'

Brett grimaced and put his arms around her as she swayed where she stood. 'It wasn't your fault. It wasn't anyone's fault. He was probably showing off. And, according to Ellen, Sasha is the more distraught of the two.'

Nicola smiled palely, but the thought of Sasha brought something else to mind. 'Marietta! Shouldn't we let her know?'

'It so happens that Marietta is on her way home.' Brett smoothed her hair with one hand. 'She rang me this morning from Singapore. She'll be up here on Saturday.'

'Oh, I thought—I didn't realise she was planning to come home! What will we do? She might have to come and stay with us. It'll be easier than coping with Chris on her own.'

'I don't think that would work,' he said after a moment, with that shade of grimness in his voice that was often associated with any mention of his ex-wife.

'But I don't mind—and she is their mother,' Nicola said.

For some reason this caused him to gaze down at her with something like a tinge of irony in his eyes, causing Nicola to chew her lip and consider that she might have been tactless. 'It's also a bit of a crisis,' she added lamely.

He smiled faintly and shrugged at the same time, as if the irony of it was apparent to him alone, then said, 'The thing is, the reason she's coming home is because she has a new man in her life.'

Nicola blinked. 'Who?' she asked dazedly.

'An oboe player. I really don't think we need to share the house with half an orchestra, even in a bit of a crisis, do you? Naturally, she's welcome to visit any time.'

Nicola closed her mouth and suddenly leant her forehead on his shoulder.

He said nothing, but held her gently, and she felt the warmth of him through his shirt, his strength that was so close, and for an instant she was tempted to break down and say simply, I love you, Brett. But the problem is, what's the use of being in love with someone who's not the slightest bit in love with you? And I could never live with what you call a real marriage if I knew it was inspired by the desire to fool Marietta into thinking you were over her.

'Nicola?'

She lifted her head. 'Sorry. Life just gets a bit complicated at times.'

'You're not wrong.' He smiled crookedly. 'Shall we take it one crisis at a time for the moment?'

'Of course.' She stiffened. 'Let's go—what am I thinking about? Poor Chris!'

It was a clean break, with no complications, and would heal quickly, the doctor assured them. They were able to take Chris home with them, his right leg encased in a plaster cast from his thigh to his toes, a few hours later.

Probably still on a high from being so much the centre of attention, Chris was putting an extremely brave face on things, but Sasha was a different matter. She couldn't do enough for her brother, and was obviously highly worked up.

'I'm not sure what's worse—to have them fighting or this,' Brett said ruefully at one stage.

Then bedtime came, and he decided to move Chris's bed into his room.

'You can sleep with me, Sash,' Nicola said quickly as Sasha looked hurt.

'Good thinking, Gunga Din,' Brett murmured, and later he came to say goodnight to them.

Sasha was asleep by this time, curled up like a kitten beside Nicola. 'She'll be better tomorrow,' Nicola whispered, and stroked Sasha's curls.

Brett said nothing, but gazed at his daughter, then lifted his hazel eyes to his wife's with a clear question in them.

'Don't worry about me. I'm fine.' Nicola swallowed. 'This isn't the—'

'The time or the place?' he finished for her, and she thought his mouth hardened briefly. But he added, 'Point taken. Sleep well.' And he closed the door quietly.

Nicola switched off the bedside lamp and cuddled up to Sasha. The thing is, she thought desolately, will there ever be a right time or place for me where you're concerned, Brett?

He took the day off work the next day, and was soon doing a jigsaw puzzle with the kids whilst Nicola helped Ellen make the beds.

For once, Ellen chose to make her feelings plain. 'Their mother,' she said darkly, having been apprised of Marietta's imminent arrival on the scene. 'Last thing we need, if you ask me. She was always good at stealing the limelight!'

Nicola made a neat nurse's corner with sheet and blanket and walked to the other side of the bed. 'She is still their mother, Ellen.'

Ellen snorted. 'Some mother. Could you have walked out on two babies? That's all they were! Mind you, I don't know why I was surprised. I saw more of them than she did after the first few months. Always at that dratted piano, she was, and never to be disturbed.'

'Lots of mothers work,' Nicola pointed out.

'Lots of mothers *have* to work, in order to put food in their mouths and a roof over their heads.'

Nicola acknowledged this with a shrug, but said, 'Can you imagine her sitting home twiddling her thumbs all day, though?'

'She'd be like a caged tiger. But you should think of these things *before* you have a family!'

Nicola sighed. 'I don't think very artistic people are like the rest of us, though. I think their art drives them—and there's not much they can do about it.'

'You're more understanding than most,' Ellen said dryly. 'Do you know what she said to him once? You probably don't; you weren't here right in the thick of things like I was. She said, "Just give me five years, Brett, that's all I need, then I'll be anything you want me to be. But if I fade out now, I'll never make it back again."' Ellen shook her head.

Nicola bent over and plumped up pillows energetically so her face was hidden. 'What did he say to that?'

But Ellen suddenly seemed to remember herself. 'Well, now,' she said awkwardly, 'I can't quite recall.'

'Ellen—' Nicola stood up and contrived to look only amused '—that's so frustrating!'

Ellen shrugged. 'He said…if her career was more important to her than he and her children were, then she had a clear choice. It or them. Of course she came back, sharp as a tack. She asked him why, and was he saying his career was more important than hers?' She smiled. 'But he got her there. He said *he* wasn't proposing to drag two small children round the world; *he* was quite happy to make a stable, solid home for them.'

Nicola smoothed the bedspread as she absorbed all of this.

'I don't think,' Ellen said slowly as she straightened with a hand to her back, 'she ever believed he'd do it, you know. But she didn't know him like I do. He's a hard man to cross.'

'I believe you,' Nicola murmured with an inward shiver.

'But there now—' Ellen's face softened '—they

couldn't be better off than they are with you. All of them,' she added somewhat cryptically, then said immediately, 'Now, what shall I make them for lunch? I know, hamburgers and chips. Why is it that kids always like the things that aren't good for them?' And she bustled away to attack the next bed.

During the afternoon Chris became fractious and tearful, so they called in their own doctor who said that it was only delayed shock and administered a mild sedative. After taking a look at Sasha—he was a father of four children himself—he did the same for her, to her intense gratification. He also suggested they hire a wheelchair for Chris until he got the hang of his crutches.

Everyone was more back to normal after an afternoon sleep.

Not that it was something she usually did, but Nicola lay down as well, and slept deeply and dreamlessly for an hour. She changed when she got up, into khaki shorts and a simple primrose cotton blouse.

Chris was delighted with his wheelchair when it arrived, and they all sat down to an early dinner together.

Richard Holloway, with a folder full of drawings under his arm, called just as they'd finished. Nicola remembered ruefully that he'd said he would, and grimaced at the short, sharp little glance Brett shot her.

'I forgot,' she said honestly.

'I think I can guess why,' Richard responded as he took in the scene. 'What have you done to yourself, old man?' he asked of Chris.

'Fell off the gym in the park and broke his leg,' Sasha supplied, while Chris swelled with importance.

'Well, now, can I be the first to sign your cast?'

And to the children's delight he not only signed the cast but drew a picture of a frog on it—because, he said, Chris would be hopping around a bit like a frog for a while. Then he drew a little girl dressed up as a nurse on the back of Sasha's hand, and she assured him she would never wash it off.

It was Brett who finally suggested to the children that this might be a good time for them to get ready for bed, and added that he had some work to do so he'd leave Richard and Nicola to it.

'No—look, I've obviously chosen a bad time,' Richard said as Brett started to wheel Chris away and Ellen cleared the table. 'I won't stay—'

'You weren't to know, and I'd like to see the plans,' Nicola broke in. 'Sit down and have a cup of coffee.'

So he did, although with an oddly thoughtful glance at Brett's retreating back.

'It's been quite a couple of days,' Nicola said ruefully as she poured the coffee.

'I can imagine.' He opened the folder and spread some pages out. 'This…' But he stopped as the doorbell rang.

Nicola frowned. 'Who on earth is this?'

It was Tara, whom Ellen showed into the family room. Tara was bearing a bunch of flowers, a gaily wrapped present and a briefcase. But, even more spectacularly, she was dressed in a black leotard, a filmy jungle print over-blouse, open down the front, and gold kid flat shoes. Her hair was once again perfect, and her make-up was full war paint. She'd switched from Chanel No 5 to Joy.

Nicola's eyes widened, and so did Richard's, for this could not have been less like the formal Tara of three nights ago. This was an unashamedly sexy version of the new litigation specialist Hinton, Harcourt had hired.

She advanced with a wide smile. 'These are for you, Nicola—' she handed over the flowers '—as a thank-you for dinner. This—' she held up the briefcase '—is for Brett. When I found out he'd rung in and asked for some briefs to be delivered here I thought *I* might as well bring them since it would give me the opportunity to discuss them with him at the same time, as well as to bring this.' She held the present aloft. 'It's for Chris, poor kid. How is he?'

'He's...he'll be fine. That's very kind of you,' Nicola said somewhat dazedly beneath this onslaught.

'Well, don't you two disturb yourselves; I'll go and find them. My...' she ran her eyes over the drawings and plans '...you do have a project going together, don't you?' she said with an oddly meaningful twinkle, and waltzed off.

Nicola clenched her teeth. 'I don't believe it!'

'A bit of a metamorphosis,' Richard commented.

'Not only that—anyone would think she owned the place. How can Brett be so *blind*?'

The little silence that followed her words caused her to flinch, then resolutely look at Richard. 'Sorry, but—' She stopped and rubbed her brow. 'Is it my imagination that she gives off unmistakable vibes to the effect that she's—interested in him?'

'No,' Richard said slowly, 'I must say I found myself wondering that the other night. She seemed to be rather subtly—well, putting herself on the same plane with him, and putting you on a lower one.'

'Thank heavens!' Nicola said fervently, and added as his eyes widened, 'I mean, I was beginning to wonder whether I was going mad. But what I can't understand is why she should imagine there's any—any hope for her. We've only just met.'

Something flickered in Richard's eyes and he looked away.

'You know something I don't?' Nicola said slowly.

He grimaced.

'Well, I know you know…what Sasha said, but is there more?' she asked.

'Nicola, I hate gossip, and—'

'No, please tell me,' she persisted.

He twined his fingers, then untwined them. 'It may be more common knowledge than you realise—oh, hell.'

He looked genuinely disturbed, then went on, 'What happened was this. If you recall, Kim was a bit stirred up the other night. And she kept on at Rod about it on the way home—did they think it was wise to have such a man-eating woman on the loose in the profession?—the kind of silly thing Kim is prone to say at times, even if she is my mother's cousin. And Rod—whether in his own defence or not, I don't know—said that if anyone should be worrying about it, it was not her but you.'

Nicola swallowed. 'Go on.'

'Of course Kim leapt on this,' he said with distaste. 'And although Rod couldn't be persuaded to say any more, she—she took to musing aloud, and said that it would make sense of the rumours she'd heard even *before* Sasha spilt the beans.'

'That this marriage was…not what it seemed?' Nicola's voice sounded strange to her own ears.

'I'm sorry,' Richard murmured. 'But it would explain why Tara is—if she's heard the rumours, too…' He gestured. 'That's assuming—' He broke off abruptly.

Nicola stared at him. 'Assuming Brett hasn't instigated it?'

'It…only crossed my mind,' he said awkwardly. 'But I wouldn't imagine he'd—well, publicly embarrass you, Nicola.'

'No,' Nicola said slowly. 'No…'

Richard sat forward. 'Can I tell you something?'

She looked at him blankly. 'There's more?'

'No. Not that I know of. This—is different.' He paused, moving his shoulders restlessly, and Nicola was suddenly gripped by a presentiment of what was to come. She swallowed, and cast around desperately for something to say. But her tongue seemed to want to cling to the roof of her mouth.

Richard finally went on, 'The thing is, I fell in love with you the moment I laid eyes on you, standing on the garden path, and if there's anything I can do, *please* let me.'

Nicola's mouth fell open, then she jumped at a sound and turned to see Brett standing in the doorway.

CHAPTER SIX

THE silence stretched, then Richard stood up and began to gather papers. 'I'll get going,' he said quietly. 'I chose a bad time.'

'Not the easiest time, no,' Brett responded, and the two men looked at each other—a steady grey glance from Richard, that wasn't exactly challenging but wasn't any kind of a backdown either, whereas Brett returned it coolly.

Then Richard said to Nicola, 'It's Saturday tomorrow. How would it be if I came back on Monday? Things might be calmer.'

'Yes. Uh—I'll—if you'd like to leave the plans I can go over them, though. Oh! I haven't had a chance to show Brett the contract yet.' She stopped, and wondered why she should sound disjointed and uncomfortable.

'No matter.' Richard smiled at her. 'Monday will do for that too.'

'I'll see you out, then,' Brett said briefly.

'Don't bother. I can find my way. Goodnight.'

'Goodnight,' she murmured, but Brett merely inclined his head.

'He wasn't to know,' she said to Brett as they heard the front door close.

Brett stirred. 'No. I—' But he broke off and swore as the front doorbell rang again. 'Bloody hell, the place is becoming like a railway station!'

But this caller didn't bother to wait to be let in, and as they both turned it was Marietta who waltzed into the dining room. 'Hi,' she said breezily. 'Couldn't wait until tomorrow to see my chickadees, so we flew up today. How are you, Nicky darling?' And she advanced to plant a kiss on Nicola's cheek.

It was at that moment that Tara entered the lounge from the opposite direction, saying, 'Brett...' and a curious little tableau ensued.

Marietta, dressed in a pink and scarlet outfit which should have clashed with her hair, let alone each colour, but which she carried off with great style and her usual vibrant beauty, blinked as her eyes fell on the other woman.

For almost a full minute they stared at each other, two mature, elegant and very sophisticated women who contrived to make Nicola, still in her khaki shorts and blouse, feel as if she hadn't left her teens. But as their gazes clashed you could almost see their hackles rising, and you could have cut the atmosphere with a knife.

Then Marietta turned to Brett and said with a jerk of her head, 'Who the hell is this?'

It was Nicola who stepped into the breach. She wasn't sure where or why she found the composure to do it, but she said gravely, 'Tara, this is Marietta, Chris and Sasha's mother. She's just arrived from overseas. And Marietta, this is Tara Wells. She's joined Hinton, Harcourt as a litigation specialist and she very kindly brought out a present for Chris because he fell and broke his leg yesterday—but he's going to be fine,' she said reassuringly.

Marietta snapped her suspicious gaze from Tara.

'Broke his leg—oh, why wasn't I here?' She looked anguished.

'That's exactly what I said; I wasn't there either. Poor Ellen had to bear the brunt of it—but why don't you go and see him?' she said warmly. 'I can guarantee it'll make him feel a hundred per cent better.'

Brett spoke for the first time. 'He is going to be fine; it's a clean break. Come.' And they walked out together.

'Tara, would you like a cup of coffee or a drink?' Nicola offered. 'I was just going to have another cup of coffee myself. It's been one of those days,' she added humorously.

Tara came out of the reverie that had held her uncharacteristically silent for so long and took her gaze from the door Marietta and Brett had gone through to rest it somewhat bemusedly on Nicola. 'I...no, thanks. I'm on my way to the gym, actually.'

'Then I'll see you out. Thanks again for the flowers and the present.'

'It...was a pleasure.'

Nicola paused in the hall after Tara had left, listening to the sounds of joyful revelry coming from Chris's bedroom, then quietly closed herself into her own bedroom.

Some time later Brett knocked on her door.

Thinking it was Marietta, she called to come in, then sat up abruptly on the ruby couch, where she'd been lying in her favourite position in her polka dot pyjamas. 'It's you.'

'Yes,' he agreed with some irony, and closed the

door. 'You didn't have to incarcerate yourself in here.'

'I wasn't.' She eyed him as he wandered over to her unicorn poster and stood staring at it with his hands shoved into the pockets of his jeans. Beneath the thin white knit of his cotton T-shirt, the set of his shoulders was tense and irritable.

'She is their mother,' she added, with a little glint of anger growing in her eyes at his words, his tone, and because he was tired and cross and there was nothing she could do about it.

'And you're their stepmother.'

'In name only,' she murmured with her own irony. 'But even so, even if I were real, I'd have left them alone.'

'You're very full of wisdom and serenity tonight, Nicola,' he said with a faint undercurrent of sarcasm as he turned to gaze at her. 'I can't help wondering if it has anything to do with Richard Holloway's declaration.'

'I thought you might have heard—'

'Oh, I heard.'

'Then you might at least,' she said swiftly and coolly, 'credit me with having absolutely no control over something that happened *before* I'd even been introduced to the man!'

'I believe we've discussed this before,' he shot back.

'No, we haven't!' she cried frustratedly, and jumped up.

'If you're contemplating slapping my face again, Nicola, don't,' he warned, and when she ground her teeth he smiled dryly and continued, 'I meant, we've discussed the fact that men tend to take one look at you and be instantly attracted. That does not necessarily mean they've fallen in love with you.'

'Well, at least he thinks he is,' she said passionately, 'whereas all you've offered me is a lot of plusses—like a checklist. Tick, tick, tick!' She gestured graphically.

'You're being childish, Nicola.'

She raised an eyebrow. 'A moment ago I was being wise and serene. But here's something for you to think about, Brett—I don't care what you think of me any longer. Because I intend to do what I see fit, and don't imagine the fact that you're my trustee will stop me.'

They stared at each other. 'And what is that?' he drawled finally.

'I...haven't decided yet.' She met his look unflinchingly, though.

'I see.' His gaze slid up and down her slim figure and lingered on the shining mass of her hair. She'd washed it and dried it with her hairdryer, so it was full of bounce and vitality. 'And very proper too,' he murmured then, with a wicked little glint in his eyes.

'If you're laughing at me, Brett—'

'Not at all,' he denied. 'I'm suitably impressed. However—and I've asked you this before—may I expect you to maintain the status quo until your twenty-first birthday?'

Nicola considered this with a frown in her eyes. 'I don't see—that's only a date. What difference does it make?'

He shrugged. 'It's looked upon as a milestone in most people's lives for some curious reason, I agree, but perhaps, as a social custom, it does mean more than an excuse to have a party.'

'Are you proposing to give me the key of the door?' she asked, somewhat sceptically.

He paused. 'On behalf of your father, Nicola,' he said at last, 'in a manner of speaking.'

There it is again, she thought dismally. We always seem to come back to my father. She sighed. 'All right. It is only a week away—although I still think it's...' She opened her hands.

'He would be relieved to know you hadn't made any momentous decisions before then.'

Nicola blinked and sniffed.

'I'm sorry,' Brett said quietly. 'I didn't mean to make you sad.'

'It's all right.' She brushed at her eyes. 'How are the kids? Is Marietta still here?'

'No. But she sang them to sleep. She's coming back tomorrow morning.'

'With...?'

'Yes. Another big day.' He grimaced. 'Mind you, as mistress of the house, you were—perfect, earlier.'

Nicola tried to stop herself, but to no avail. She started to smile, then she started to laugh, and when he took her hand in his she didn't resist. 'Have you ever seen two people take such an instantaneous dislike to each other?'

'No,' he responded with a look of rueful amusement, and kissed her knuckles. 'Will you sleep all right now?'

She looked up into his eyes, and the smile on her lips wavered and died. 'I guess so,' she said huskily. 'Will you?' She bit her lip and looked away.

'So long as I know the mistress of my house is comfortable and reassured, yes. Look at me, Nicola.'

'Brett,' she said on a breath, 'I'm fine.'

'Nicola.'

She hesitated, then lifted her lashes uncertainly, 'What?'

Something flickered in his eyes, but she couldn't read it. He said, 'I just wanted to tell you that in all the drama earlier you were so…nice, so sane, your father would have been very proud of you.'

'Now you are going to make me cry,' she said helplessly.

'No.' He took her loosely in his arms. 'You should feel proud too.'

She shook her head, but felt the emotion gripping her begin to subside. 'I don't think I should fall into that trap, actually,' she said with a grin. 'I'm sure the Reverend Callam would tell you pride comes before a fall—although he did have some rather un-Christian notions for a—' She stopped.

'Who is the Reverend Callam?' he queried quizzically.

'Uh…' Nicola mused regretfully that she should always *think* before she spoke. 'Well…' She hesitated, but encountered a look in Brett's hazel eyes that was at the same time patient yet fully expectant of receiving an answer. 'Oh, well, he was the marriage counsellor I went to see.'

One eyebrow shot up as Brett reviewed this piece of information, then he looked at her searchingly. 'What un-Christian notions did he put into your head?'

'Nothing terrible, just—I guess you could call it something to do with human nature, that's all.'

'The mind boggles,' he said dryly. 'Nicola—'

'No, I'm not going to elaborate,' Nicola said firmly, 'so don't waste your breath, Brett. It…it's nothing for you to worry about.'

For a moment he remained unimpressed, then a glint of devilry gleamed in his eyes. 'That's usually my line.'

She smiled faintly. 'Perhaps a bit of role reversal wouldn't do us any harm.'

'Does that mean you're about to lecture me on the error of my ways?' The devilry was still there, although his expression was grave.

'No. But it can't hurt to put yourself in someone else's shoes occasionally,' she said tartly.

'Indeed it can't,' he replied softly, and ran one hand absently up the back of her neck beneath the fall of her hair. 'Although I wonder if you've ever tried to put yourself in mine?'

Nicola said nothing as two things struck her with unusual force and a sense of poignancy. How many times had she tried to do just that? she wondered. Only to be met by a seemingly impenetrable barrier. And secondly, had he any idea how fragile her neck felt with his hand curved about it, and how the feel of it sent ripples of awareness flowing through her body?

Not only that, it opened up channels of thought, as well as the trickles of arousal running through her. How different, for example, this embrace was from the one three nights ago, with its exchange of hostilities and that electric spark that had flamed between them. How much warmer this felt, and how those channels of her mind were passing messages to her senses.

So that she observed and thought about little things, like the lines beside his mouth, which she'd always loved, and felt her fingertips tingle with an urge to touch them. It was the same with his hair, brown, crisp and clean, giving off chestnut glints beneath the ceiling light, and the darker tips of his eyelashes, and the shape of his chin—which Sasha had inherited, despite the overall look of her mother. A chin which, when she tilted it, left no doubt that she could be quite as determined as her father.

Then there was the fact that to be so close to him in this tranquil way was to be able to breathe in the scent of him and find it fascinating and different.

Just pure man scent, I guess, she thought, with a touch of clean cotton from his T-shirt. Do I have a pure woman scent? she wondered. Or has it been drowned beneath shampoo, conditioner and scented soap? What would it be like to lie on a bed with him? Her thoughts ran on, down a familiar path. To be undressed and to feel his hands run over my skin, to be made love to...

'Nicola?'

She blinked. 'Yes?'

'What were you thinking?'

'Nothing much,' she answered slowly.

'It didn't look like it.'

Don't *blush,* she warned herself, and shrugged slightly—a delicate disclaimer.

But their gazes locked—she found she couldn't

look away as his eyes probed the depths of hers. 'You looked,' he said, 'surprised and—assessing.'

'I did?'

'But not unpleasantly surprised. And thoughtful as well.'

She moved at last, and he took his hand away from her neck but kept her within the circle of his arms. 'That's quite a combination of looks,' she said wryly, but her heart was beating strangely, and she was very much afraid he would see it in the pulse at the base of her throat.

But he said easily, 'Going to tell me?'

She chewed her lip. 'No.'

'So it's something else I don't need to worry about?'

'No. I mean, no, you don't have to worry,'

He raised an amused eyebrow. 'I'd still rather know.'

'Brett, don't be difficult,' she protested. 'It...wasn't anything much.'

'All the more reason not to want to hide it from me,' he countered mildly but he tilted his chin that Sasha had inherited.

She clicked her tongue frustratedly. 'You're impossible. All *right*, but don't blame me if you don't like it. I was wondering—just as a natural impulse— what it would be like if we...made love, that's all.'

'*All?*'

'Well—' she tilted her own chin '—it was something you yourself suggested only the day before yesterday, and this is a...a fairly intimate position to be in with you, I guess—that's why it came to mind. If men can be men, girls probably have the same problem sometimes—don't say it,' she warned, unable to stem the flood of colour that came to her cheeks this time, although her eyes were sapphire-blue and imperious.

'How the hell do you know what I was going to say?' he asked roughly.

'I'm sure I've heard it before.' She gazed at him defiantly. '"Don't be childish, Nicola." Or that other gem—"You're testing your powers of attraction, Nicola!"'

He released her abruptly. 'And you don't think it's either of those things?'

'I think,' she said, with a great effort at control, although her heart was hurting, 'that you shouldn't put me in these unfilial positions with you when all you see yourself as is standing in for my father.'

He swore, and she took a step backwards at the blazing, almost murderous expression in his eyes and the hard, white line of his mouth. 'You seem to forget who started this,' he ground out, then swung on his heel and walked out.

Nicola stared at the door and put her hands to her mouth. What have I *done*? she asked herself, and sank down onto the ruby couch. But isn't it true? Even if I did start it? Why, oh, why, did I ever…?

It was a long time before she fell asleep. Not only because she felt thoroughly miserable, and as if she'd destroyed something precious, but also confused. How could he not know how she felt in his arms? Did he really feel absolutely nothing himself, and—if so—why accuse her of having started it—started what? A purely physical reaction in a man who felt nothing more for her?

She moved unhappily and wished she had Sasha to cuddle, but Sasha had obviously been reassured by her mother, which led Nicola to think of Marietta, and that tense little stand-off between her and Tara.

Why would two women take such a dislike to each other on sight? There had to be a common denominator and it had to be Brett, didn't it? she asked herself. She was quite sure in her own mind that Tara had divined the state of their marriage somehow, be it gossip, rumour or whatever, and had her own agenda in mind for Brett. Was that what Marietta had divined? And, if so, did she resent it on Nicola's behalf…or on her own?

She turned over, then sat up and pulled her pillow into her arms as another scenario took shape in her mind. Assuming Marietta had known all along that this was a marriage of convenience, did it suit her own ends, if she had plans to try to win Brett back after five years? Had she seen it as a way of keeping him free from other women, of ensuring the children were happy? And just possibly, knowing Marietta, Nicola thought with some wryness, as a way of keeping *me* out of harm's way?

But what about this boyfriend? A double-barrelled attempt to get Brett back? Make him jealous in other words?

Oh, no! *Dear* Reverend Callam, if only you knew what a can of worms you opened up. Well, is it any wonder I can't think straight?

She couldn't help thinking with some irony that it was an uncomfortable household she was mistress of the next morning.

Brett was cooler than she'd ever known him, and she couldn't help flinching and feeling chilled to the bone on the odd occasions when his inscrutable hazel gaze fell on her. The children picked up these vibes unerringly, and were correspondingly difficult. Chris demanded to know how he was going to be able to do *anything* with this horrible thing on his leg, and Sasha decided she had to wear her favourite dress for Mummy and her visitor.

'You can't, darling. Remember you spilt raspberry cordial all down the front? Well, we couldn't get the stain out, I'm afraid.'

Sasha burst into tears.

'Don't be such a baby, Sasha,' Brett said coldly. 'You have a million other dresses to wear.'

'But I like that dress, and Mummy sent it to me from America,' Sasha wept.

'I'm sure she'll understand,' Nicola said soothingly.

'Why do girls make such a fuss about clothes?' Chris asked disdainfully. 'Just be happy you don't have to wear this!' He tapped his cast. 'Then you'd really have something to cry about.'

'I hate you, Chris,' Sasha panted, scarlet in the face. 'I—'

'That'll do,' Brett ordered, and wheeled Chris out of the room. 'I expect to see you dressed and ready in ten minutes—in whatever Nicola decides you should wear, Sash,' he added over his shoulder.

'Why's Daddy being so horrible this morning?' Sasha asked tearfully, and clutched Nicola's hand.

Not sure whether she wanted to laugh or cry, Nicola made a sudden decision—she just didn't have the moral fortitude to endure the rest of this day. She helped Sasha choose another dress, then took her into her own bedroom where she cajoled the little girl into a better humour by spraying some perfume on her, tucking one of her own lace-edged hankies into her pocket and tying back her red-brown curls with one of her own ribbons. But she also picked up her bag on the way out.

'Going somewhere?' Brett asked curtly as she delivered Sasha to the den, where he was playing cards with Chris.

'Yes. I don't think you'll need me today,' she murmured.

'Where?'

Nicola glanced at him briefly. 'Just out. I'll be home for dinner. Now, Sasha and Chris, Mummy will be here soon, and in the meantime I want you to be especially nice to Daddy—see if you can get him in better mood!' And she kissed their heads, shot Brett a faintly malicious little look and left before anyone could protest.

But it was a long, lonely day.

She went to the Pier Markets and spent an hour browsing through the second-hand bookstalls, bumping into a couple of Brett's clients, who expressed surprise that she should be on her own. She explained, with a feeling of discomfort, that she was just having a day out. Then she decided to see a movie, but that still left her with several hours to kill.

She thought longingly of her flying lessons, but her instructor was still away on holiday. She called to see a girlfriend, but she was out.

She had a Vienna coffee at a café overlooking the Marlin Marina, and waved hello to two lawyers from another firm as she watched the cruise and dive boats coming back from Green Island, Fitzroy, Michaelmas Cay and Arlington Reef. And finally, as the sun slipped down the sky, she drove home.

The house seemed to be unnaturally quiet as she put her key into the front door, although Brett's car was in the garage.

'Ellen?' she called tentatively, and remembered that it was Saturday and Ellen's afternoon off.

Then she jumped as Brett appeared soundlessly in the lounge doorway. He was barefoot and wearing only shorts. 'Oh! I thought there was no one here.'

'There isn't, apart from me.'

Her eyes widened. 'Where are they?'

'Gone to spend the night with Marietta.'

'But...but...'

'They'll be fine. In fact, in all the turmoil, we forgot that we needed a babysitter tonight.'

Nicola blinked, and realised he must have just had a swim or a shower. His hair was wet and droplets gleamed on his shoulders. 'A...? Oh, no! The law society ball! I did forget. But surely we won't go.'

He propped his shoulders against the doorframe. 'Not if we were worried about Chris, but he's perfectly happy to spend the night with his mother.'

Nicola hesitated, then walked into the kitchen, where she dropped her bag onto the island counter beside the chrysanthemum, and poured herself a glass of water.

Brett followed her. 'Can you think of any other reason for us not to go?'

Nicola didn't turn immediately, because this was the same hard, cool Brett of the morning and she had no idea how to deal with him.

She drew a breath, swallowed, and swung round. 'A couple,' she said quietly. 'I don't feel like going to a ball tonight, and I don't feel that there's any point in us going as Mr and Mrs Harcourt because I'm quite sure I couldn't hold up my end of this…farce. I'm equally sure you either hate me, actively dislike me or thoroughly disapprove of me—all ingredients for an unpleasant evening, don't you agree?'

'No, I don't,' he said curtly. 'So get your glad rags out, Nicola, because we are going.'

She gasped. 'You can't make me, Brett. Go on your own, if you're so set on it. Make some excuse for me—say I'm sick—or go with Tara! I'm sure she'd be delighted.'

'Nicola.' He closed in on her. 'These continual and childish references to Tara don't become you. It so happens I *have* to go because I'm delivering the address. It's also too late to prevent there being an embarrassing gap at my side, and because my ex-wife happens to be in town it could cause talk and speculation. Particularly if you've been drifting around town on your own all day. Don't forget,' he said sardonically, 'this place is not that big.'

It hit home like an arrow as she recalled the clients she'd bumped into earlier, and the two lawyers. All the same, she said tautly, with her face pale and furious, 'Do you think I care, Brett? Actually, if you like *I'll* go and babysit your children—after all, a babysitter is all I am really—why don't you *take* your ex-wife!'

'Don't be ridiculous,' he said scathingly. 'She's the last person on earth I'd take.'

Nicola opened her mouth and closed it abruptly as a medley of confused thoughts ran through her mind—what had happened here today? Something that had prompted this? Something to do with Marietta and her boyfriend? Did Brett need to make some kind of a statement to the world tonight? But...

She looked up into his eyes, but all she could see was a kind of tough determination. Her shoulders slumped and she said tonelessly, 'All right. What time?'

'Seven. We'll leave here at half past six. That—' he glanced at his watch '—gives you an hour. Long enough?'

'Yes, Brett.' She marched away.

There were several suitable gowns hanging in her walk-in wardrobe—the law society ball was a very formal, black tie function—and her hand hovered before she drew out one. But it was still a race against time as she painted her nails, showered and dealt with her hair and make-up. And it was with a buzzing mind that she got through it all, because something told her that things had gone wrong—more wrong than they'd been before, if that was possible.

But finally she stepped out of her bedroom and found Brett on the terrace, consulting his watch. It was six-thirty on the dot.

'Well?' she said. 'I'm here.'

He turned slowly and studied her critically. The pool lights were on and the barbecue pavilion was lit up. The dress was candy-floss pink and covered in sequins, which reflected the soft lighting. It clung to her figure, had a low back and was supported by two narrow straps. Her sandals were high, silver and also sequinned, and her purse was silver mesh. She wore her pearl bracelet, her hair was swept up in a pleat and she had on a pair of square pearl drop-earrings.

'I see you're not taking Chris's advice tonight,' he murmured at last.

'No.'

'On the other hand, he didn't get it quite right. You look lovely, if a little severe.'

'That could be because I *feel* a little severe. Shall we get this over and done with?' She turned to go in.

'Nicola.'

She set her lips and turned back. In a black dinner suit, with a snow-white starched shirt-front and black tie, Brett Harcourt was a commanding figure, enough to make her heart jolt, but she refused to allow her expression to change.

He smiled unexpectedly. 'I wasn't being critical.'

She shrugged, then blinked as lightning lit the sky and a faint rumble of thunder made itself heard.

'We might need an umbrella,' he added, after a moment, and raised a hand to fiddle with the shoulder strap of her gown.

She looked away and didn't see the frown in his eyes as they rested on her. She was too conscious of the suddenly electric tension the feel of his fingers on her skin was producing in her, so that her heart started to beat oddly and her pulses raced. But she forced herself to breathe deeply, and when she raised her eyes to his, they were noncommittal.

His lips twisted. 'Well, it will do the garden good.'

'Yes.'

He took his hand away and bowed for her to pre-cede him with a faintly sardonic gleam in his eye. She walked through the house to the garage to find that the BMW already had its hood up, and she got in, handling her skirt carefully. It was a completely silent drive into town and the new Convention Centre.

'Hello, Tara,' she said about an hour later, when they'd sat down to dinner. Tara was at their table. She was with another lawyer from Hinton, Harcourt, but it was obvious the pairing was only to make the num-bers even. Tara glowed in a filmy, layered chartreuse gown.

'How's Chris?' she asked immediately.

'A little disturbed about how he's going to do *any-thing* with that horrible thing on his leg.' Nicola smiled ruefully and sipped champagne.

'I'm surprised you came tonight,' Tara said. 'I thought you might have had your hands full.'

Nicola considered that and discovered she was sud-denly impervious to this woman's needling—or what-ever it was. 'Thanks for your concern, but Marietta's taken over,' she said easily. 'I love your gown, by the way. Did you get it in Cairns?'

Tara looked vaguely taken aback by the genuine-ness of Nicola's tone, and Brett, who had sat silent through this exchange, flicked his wife a sudden glance.

'No, Brisbane,' Tara said. 'I was going to say the same of yours,' she added somewhat lamely.

'Thanks.' Nicola took another sip of champagne

and turned to Brett as the band started to play. 'Shall we dance, darling?'

'If…you want to be the first on the floor,' he responded with a narrow little look.

'Why not? Oh, and it's a samba! We do that rather well together, don't we?'

He hesitated for a moment, then pushed back his chair.

They did it so well together they were the cynosure of all eyes as her dress shimmered under the lights and her natural sense of rhythm gave her fluency and grace. The band was obviously delighted, so they prolonged the number.

'What are you doing, Nicola?' Brett said as they came together—and parted.

'What you wanted me to do,' she answered as they came together—and parted.

'As in making a spectacle of us?'

'Not at all.' But she glanced up at him over her shoulder, as he put his hands round her waist from behind her, to see that he was looking down at her enigmatically.

She returned his look with a mysterious little one of her own. Then she spun away with the music and said whimsically when they came together again, 'Don't worry, I won't attack you and kiss you! I'm just allaying all talk and speculation, and any embarrassment for you. Besides,' she added honestly, 'I just love to samba—and you *were* the one who taught me, Brett!'

He said no more, and they finally left the floor to a storm of applause.

'My dear Nicola.' It was Rod Mason, who took her

hand, then enveloped her in a bear hug. 'You are a thing of joy and beauty to watch!' He released her and turned to Brett. 'You're a lucky dog, old man!'

'Don't I know it,' Brett replied, and if there was a faint undercurrent in his voice only Nicola seemed to notice it.

'Never mind, darling, I'll behave myself from now on,' she said to him, and patted his lapel.

'You must admit,' he said *sotto voce*, as they started on their entrée, 'that this mood is a little different from the one you left home in.'

'I'm probably being childish—well, girlish.' She smiled at him. 'Or just plain naughty?' she added as an afterthought.

'Determined to fling all my sins in my face?' he said dryly.

'You were the one who insisted I come. But before this degenerates into a slanging match,' she responded swiftly, 'and undoes all the good I've done—although I have no real idea *why* I had to do it—you should have the next dance with Tara.'

'Oh—why?'

'Because—' she eyed him impishly '—I intend to dance with everyone at the table while I've got this music in my soul. In fact, in lieu of being able to work anything out, and because the only other thing I can think of doing is going to Tibet to get away from it all…' she looked rueful '…I don't see why I shouldn't enjoy myself!'

It started as a look of surprise in his eyes, then became an unwilling salute, and finally he laughed softly. 'Point taken. There are times when you're unique, you know.'

She looked away, and to her horror heard herself say, 'Not unique enough for you, though.'

'Nicola—'

'Don't. Sorry, I didn't mean that—uh—it must be the champagne. Oh, look who's here. Richard. Don't worry, though, I'll be very discreet—and I certainly won't dance the samba with him.'

He gazed down at her steadily, but the expression in his eyes suddenly struck her as being bleak, even filled with pain for a moment, before he looked away.

It was as if a hand had squeezed her heart. She didn't know what would cause him to look like that, but she was pretty sure she could guess—it had to be Marietta and the new man in her life.

And here I am, playing the fool, adding to his problems... She closed her eyes briefly and said, barely audibly, 'Brett?'

He looked down at her again, searchingly.

'Sorry—that's all. I *am* being girlish. I'll—don't worry about me this evening. I'll be...I won't cause any problems.'

What he would have said she never knew, because, with a drumroll, the leader of the band announced that the speeches were due to begin and invited Brett to take the rostrum.

Throughout his speech, even though the lights were dimmed, Nicola, without turning her head, could see Tara's rapt expression and the unconscious, sheer admiration the other woman couldn't hide. For her own part, she found she couldn't concentrate on what Brett was saying, because running through her mind were all the Bretts she knew—not just this polished man of the world, who spoke with a mixture of authority and humour.

Brett with the children. Brett on the beach. Brett with her, before she'd destroyed the balance of their relationship. Brett hurting because, as she'd always known, he could never forget Marietta—even though he might tell himself it had all burnt out.

Is that why Tara has ceased to get to me? she wondered. How can I get him to understand that Marietta, without knowing it, might just have taken the Reverend Callam's advice? I'm sure it's got to be that! What if I go and see her...?

She realised suddenly that his speech had ended and he was coming back to the table—and she was the only one not applauding enthusiastically.

She started to clap belatedly, then he was beside her, sitting down, looking wry.

Tara immediately leant over to congratulate him. 'Well said, Brett! I particularly liked the bit about...'

Nicola grimaced inwardly and switched off—in a manner of speaking. In fact, so much so, he had to touch her arm to bring her back.

'Oh. Sorry,' she murmured.

'You looked as if you were a million miles away.'

'No...'

'Would you like to go?'

Her eyes widened. 'Wouldn't that...? No, I'm fine. Why?' she asked uncertainly.

'I'm not enjoying myself much either.'

She studied him, then slipped her hand over his. 'A bit later. It would look strange.'

He transferred his gaze down to her fingers on his and said, 'You're right. OK, let's soldier on.'

So they did. But the effort, on top of an aimless, unhappy day, told on Nicola, and she fell asleep in the car on the way home, only to half wake up and find that he'd carried her into her bedroom.

'Sorry,' she mumbled.

He handed Nicola her pyjamas and paused. 'Can you manage?' he said quietly at last.

'Of course, but thanks.'

'Goodnight, then.'

And she was alone, suddenly wide awake, staring at the door as he closed it quietly behind him.

CHAPTER SEVEN

IT WAS pouring with rain the next morning, and cool.

Nicola got up reluctantly and looked out to sea, but the horizon was obscured and the whole world looked grey and bleak. She shivered and pulled on a brave yellow tracksuit, which helped to warm her body but did not release any burst of inspiration in her mind.

Then the utter silence of the house struck her again. Of course—it was Ellen's day off, as well as there being no children in residence, but when she glanced at her watch to see that it was nine o'clock, she frowned. Brett was not that late a sleeper, even on Sundays.

Nor was he this Sunday, she discovered, for his car was gone. Then she saw a note on the fridge from him, saying that one of his clients had got himself into trouble and he was at the watch-house with him.

She crumpled it up and threw it into the garbage bin, then absently made herself a boiled egg for breakfast. As she ate she went through the kaleidoscope of memories of the night before. Three things stood out. The half-formulated idea of going to see Marietta and trying to explain how things stood, the foolish words she'd uttered about not being unique enough for him, and...

But the third was the most vivid mental image she carried. Despite her sleepiness the night before, when Brett had carried her from the car to the bedroom, it

141

had shouted itself to her that he, once he'd put her down, was determined not to lay a finger on her.

All the more reason I should do something, she thought, and brushed a stray tear away.

She did a few chores after her breakfast, but in a half-hearted fashion. It was as she was tidying Brett's bedroom that she heard his car. She hesitated, then went on making the bed.

She heard him come through the connecting door to the garage, heard what sounded like the kettle being filled and was nerving herself to go and greet him when he appeared at the bedroom doorway.

'Hi,' she said uncertainly, straightening. 'Got your note. Is he in serious trouble?'

Brett wore jeans, boots and a pale grey jumper. His hair was ruffled and damp and his eyes bleak. 'Serious enough. He threatened to shoot both his wife and himself if she persisted in leaving him for another man. He was only restrained in the nick of time.'

Nicola gasped. 'Who is it? Do I know him?'

Brett told her who it was and she did know him. 'But that's incredible—he's not that kind of man,' she protested.

'Who knows *what* we're really like under the surface?' he said dryly. 'Who knows, for example—? Oh, what the hell.' He strode over to his veranda door and slammed it shut, then stood staring at the rain through the glass panels moodily.

'Brett,' she said after a long moment, then paused to marshal her thoughts and choose the right track to approach him in this mood. 'Brett—' She stopped and looked around.

This was the bedroom he and Marietta had shared, and he'd changed nothing, not the king-size four-poster bed, with its glorious coverlet of rich forest-green quilted silk—a colour that had suited Marietta perfectly—nor had he changed the gold-braided head roll pillows, the gold foil lampshades or the fuchsia-framed paintings on the white walls.

'Brett—that was the kettle. Would you like a cup of coffee?'

He shrugged, as if it didn't matter much to him.

'Come into the lounge; I'll bring it through.'

She made a plunger pot of Blue Mountain coffee and put out some of Ellen's home-made biscuits.

'What I was going to say...' she eyed him as she poured the coffee; he was sprawled out on one of the settees with his hands behind his head '...was this. We do have...something between us, don't we?'

He didn't respond.

'I mean, we are friends, if nothing else, and we've been through a bit together, haven't we? I think losing my father affected you greatly as well. And we... always put Sasha and Chris first—that kind of thing, so—'

He sat up abruptly. 'So? What's this leading up to, Nicola?'

She shivered inwardly, because his eyes were hard and cold, but she found she was determined not to be scared off. She got up to carry his cup over to him, then sat down again. 'It's leading up to this—won't you please tell me what happened yesterday? Even if I can't help I'll probably understand, and it *might* just help to tell someone.'

'Understand?' he repeated sardonically, and scanned her troubled expression, her brave yellow tracksuit and the faint blue shadows under her eyes. 'Nicola...' He looked away and his shoulders slumped. 'There are some things I hope you never understand.'

She chewed her lip. 'Then I can't be much of a friend in your eyes, Brett. And I guess you still regard me as a child.' There was a faintly mocking little glint in her blue eyes and her chin was tilted dangerously.

'All right,' he said harshly. 'What do you make of this? Marietta is using this new man in her life—who, incidentally, is younger than she is but besotted with her—to point out to me the pitfalls our children are going to encounter if we don't remarry. You see, her days of touring the world to perform are over, and she intends to settle in Sydney—she's been offered a teaching post at the Conservatorium of Music and a guest spot with the Sydney Symphony Orchestra for the next three years.'

'But *why*? I mean, she's at her peak! She's world-famous.'

'She's also suffering from RSI. She has to cut down or it could get to the stage where she could never play again.'

'Oh, no,' Nicola said painfully. 'How will she cope? But—the other night...' She gestured and frowned. 'There was no sign that she's taken a blow like this. She was her normal—her—'

'Her normal ebullient, outrageous self,' Brett commented dryly.

'Well, she was!'

He stared down at her. 'That's because she's

switched obsessions,' he said grimly. 'You, of all people, must know how good she is at doing that.'

'Switched—? You mean...' Nicola swallowed '...to recreating your marriage?'

'Precisely. Only, in typical Marietta fashion, she's doing it in a below-the-belt fashion.'

A vision of the Reverend Callam's face swam through Nicola's mind, and of the way Richard Holloway had fallen, unwittingly, into a scheme of things that could also be described as 'below the belt'. She shuddered inwardly this time. 'That's...that's... I don't know what to say.'

He smiled unamusedly. 'I thought you might not. But it's not going to happen.'

'Is it a good idea for Sasha and Chris to be—exposed to this, though?' She flinched at his cutting little look.

'As you keep pointing out to me, she is their mother,' he said with irony. 'And I would imagine the trauma of me trying to withhold them from her could be equally damaging.'

'But what's he like? The oboe player?'

Brett shrugged and grimaced. 'If you met him in other circumstances, you'd probably like him. A gentle giant—and he's very good with kids. They took to him immensely.'

'Oh, Brett,' she said softly, and with a wealth of compassion in her voice.

'Don't,' he said with sudden violence. 'The last thing I need from you is—sympathy.'

She stood up as her face paled, and she whispered, 'Why?' Then she stiffened and turned, as if to run from the room.

'Nicola—Nicola.' He was on his feet swiftly and reached for her. 'Don't. I'm *sorry*. I...' He stared down at her.

She saw that he was pale too, but she said huskily, 'Let me go, Brett. It doesn't matter—'

'Yes, it does.' He gathered her close and buried his face in her hair. She felt all the tension in his muscles, then the sudden, involuntary slackening of them, and he raised his head, looked into her eyes briefly, and started to kiss her.

Shock held her immobile. Then she jumped as he pushed his hands beneath her tracksuit top. They were cold and hard on her skin, but their movement was gentle, as if he was trying to warm them on her, and a flood of feeling ran through her—desire, but not only that. A yearning to offer him the warmth he so obviously needed, physically as well as emotionally. Sympathy, yes, but so much more.

Oh, Brett, don't do this to me, she thought. You *can't* make me a substitute for Marietta.

But none of her anguish was proof against the increasingly hungry way he kissed her.

Nothing could erase her own hunger as he tapped it right to its source, with his hands unerringly moving to the most sensitive parts of her body. Slipping beneath her bra to touch her breasts and tease her nipples to tight little peaks. Sliding beneath her tracksuit pants and cupping her hips, then moving beneath the elastic of her bikini briefs, holding her hard against him and kissing not only her mouth but her throat while she clung to him dizzily and her body, her very core, revealed to him all that he did to her.

She had no idea what made him raise his head suddenly, and made his hands go still. Then she heard it herself—car doors closing, voices, children.

Shock etched itself in her eyes and she all but fell as he released her. He immediately steadied her with his hands around her waist, but she went paler than she'd ever been before and could only stare at him, horrified.

He swore softly. 'Nicola, don't look like that, I'm *sorry*.'

She licked her swollen lips. 'I... I...' But nothing more would come out.

His face tightened as the doorbell pealed. 'It's OK, I locked it,' he murmured. 'We've got a few moments—we've got all the time in the world.'

'But I feel...' I feel like a pawn in this game between you and Marietta—but then I always was, wasn't I? she thought despairingly, and abruptly pushed herself away from him. 'No, we haven't,' she said starkly. 'You go. I'll just tidy myself up...' And she spun suddenly on her heel and ran for the safety and seclusion of her bedroom.

She had a shower—anything to delay the inevitable—and this time dressed with more care. She chose fine caramel cord trousers and a long-sleeved thin wool sweater in a misty jacaranda-blue with a plain round neck. She tucked the sweater in and added a thin, plaited gold leather belt to the pants. She put her locket on, then rummaged through her drawers and found a jacaranda and beige silk scarf which she tied around her neck jauntily.

Then she brushed her hair until it shone and fell like a river of pale gold to below her shoulders—and turned her attention to her face. She never used much make-up, but this seemed to be an occasion for it. Anything to draw attention away from the still stunned look in her eyes, the fact that she was unusually pale.

Ten minutes later she was satisfied. The lightest touch of foundation and some judicious use of blusher had done the trick. She added mascara to her lashes and stood back, then reached for Chris's despised perfume but put it down almost at once. Enough was enough, and what was she trying to do anyway? she wondered. Upstage Marietta? When had that ever been possible? she thought sadly.

She was searching for a pair of shoes to complete the outfit when Sasha came to find her—a Sasha brimming with excitement but also saying that they'd *missed* her.

It touched her heart, and the hug Chris gave her did the same. Then she couldn't put off greeting Marietta—a Marietta once again brimming with vitality and looking marvellous in black suede culottes, high-heeled boots and a suede waistcoat over a bottle-green shirt, her flaming hair tied back with a green velvet ribbon. Marietta was exactly the same as she'd always been. Nicola wondered what she'd expected.

'Did you have a nice night, Nicky? I always used to enjoy the law society ball. It gave me great pleasure to wow the pants off them—as you may remember?' Marietta turned to Brett with a mischievous look.

But Brett was watching *her*, Nicola saw, and made no comment. In fact he looked tall, withdrawn and impatient.

'Funny you should say that,' Nicola found her

tongue suddenly. 'I treated them to a samba last night they haven't seen the likes of for years. I got a standing ovation.'

Why she said it, she wasn't sure. She could never equate Marietta with the likes of Tara Wells, never indulge in a round of tit-for-tat with the mother of Brett's children—so why? Because she'd never been good at feeling sadly and righteously misused and wasn't about to start? Probably. She shrugged inwardly and turned to the large young man standing behind Chris's wheelchair. 'Please introduce me, Marietta?'

'Darling, this is Ralph Metcalfe. Isn't he gorgeous?'

Ralph actually blushed, and Nicola, studying him critically, decided that he was. He wore a round-necked T-shirt under a trendy tweed jacket with jeans. He was very tall, and in his middle twenties, she judged. He had long blond hair, a physique that would have done the Chippendales proud and features that could have been hewn out of stone. Slightly at variance with them, though, was a pair of soft and friendly blue eyes.

Nicola blinked, and Ralph said with a sweet, shy smile, 'I believe you play the harp?'

'I do. And you're an oboist?'

'Cor anglais, actually.' He had a decidedly English accent, and he went on with great feeling, 'Mellower, sadder and much more mysterious, don't you think?'

'Don't start him off,' Marietta intervened with a grin. 'Ralph, this is Nicola—Brett's second wife. Contrary to all the norms, we're very fond of each other.'

'I'm glad,' Ralph said fervently. 'I abhor unease and upheaval when it's so much easier to love each other.' But he studied Nicola with some surprise, her slim figure, lovely hair, the smooth skin and dark blue eyes, then glanced at Brett, almost as if saluting him.

'Yes, well,' Brett said, moving his shoulders restlessly as Nicola struggled with an insane desire to laugh, 'thanks very much for babysitting—'

'We're not babies any more, Daddy,' Sasha protested, although affectionately, and took his hand to rub the back of it against her cheek. 'Mummy says we've grown up so much in the past few months, she can't believe it.' And she reached for Marietta's hand too.

Brett looked down at her, and Nicola stared at the three of them, linked together. It struck her like a flash of lightning that for Chris and Sasha's sake she could no longer muddle along. If Marietta wanted to come back then at least she wouldn't have Nicola to climb over. Nor, for that matter, was any flower-power cor anglais player going to get in the way—and, even if she had to personally ram it home to her, neither was Tara.

The speed with which this flashed through her mind was almost equalled by the inventiveness that followed. 'Ralph,' she said, 'I…uh…would love to show you a bit of Cairns. And I'm sure Brett and Marietta need some time alone with Sasha and Chris—oh, and look, the sun's trying to come out! Shall we go for a drive?'

'Nicky—'

'Nicola—'

Brett and Marietta spoke together—Marietta in tones of utter surprise, Brett roughly.

But she smiled at them both. 'Don't worry, I'll take good care of him,' she said to Marietta, and, squaring her shoulders, turned to Brett. 'Things can't go on like this,' she said very quietly. 'Please, you two need to talk.'

Then she took Ralph's hand and drew him out of the room.

'She didn't tell me,' Ralph Metcalfe said dazedly.

They were having lunch at Palm Cove, beneath a white sail umbrella on a green lawn that led to the beach. The sun had succeeded in coming out, although the day was still on the cool side—for Cairns. Double Island looked to be only a stone's throw away, across the glittering waters of the cove.

Nicola had ordered Barramundi fillets in a beer batter and a Caesar salad, while Ralph was eating a very large rump steak. They'd ordered a bottle of wine and Nicola, although she'd felt like pinching herself to think that she should be explaining these things to a complete stranger, had described how her marriage to Brett was only a marriage of convenience.

'What does it all mean?' He stared at her bewilderedly.

Nicola paused, then said delicately, 'How—well do you know her?'

'We've…we've been together for two weeks. But I've worshipped her from afar for a lot longer,' he said, with no trace of embarrassment. He took a sip of wine. 'Not that she'll let me sleep with her, but I can wait. I mean, she wouldn't have suggested coming all this way with her if—well, if it wasn't going to happen some time.' But he looked at her wistfully, and uncertainly.

Nicola touched his hand briefly. 'That's what I was afraid of, Ralph. You see, I'm pretty sure I was a...stopgap—while Marietta had to be overseas so much and Brett refused to have that kind of a marriage. And now I'm pretty sure you're...well, she's using you to make him jealous. You wouldn't like that, would you?'

He took a few moments to think his way through this. 'No. But why can't they...? Why all this trauma?'

'Two *very* strong characters, Ralph,' Nicola said briskly, then sighed. 'Love is often not that simple, is it?'

'Don't tell me,' he said moodily. 'For example, can you explain to me why I'm always attracted to older women who very often have husbands or exes or bloody careers?'

'This has happened to you before, Ralph?' Nicola asked sympathetically.

'It has,' he said intensely. 'It keeps happening to me. What do you think she planned to do with me when she got her damned husband back?' He looked around, as if he'd suddenly realised he'd been dumped on an alien planet.

Nicola chewed her lip and sent up a fervent little prayer that she'd got this right—otherwise...well, she couldn't bear to think about it. 'Perhaps,' she said slowly, dodging the question, 'you should try younger women. Although not me,' she added hastily as his blue eyes rested on her with a suddenly speculative gleam in them. 'I'm…spoken for. But there must—I mean, you're such a hunk—there must be millions of…' she rushed on, and someone tapped her on the shoulder.

She turned convulsively, expecting Brett or Marietta, but it was Tara.

She swore audibly and said, 'Tara, you frightened the life out of me! What are *you* doing here!'

'If you can come to Palm Cove for lunch on a Sunday, why can't I?' Tara said aggressively. 'But shouldn't you be home with your *family*?' she added venomously. 'Instead of lunching with strange men— does Brett know about this?' She eyed Ralph with extreme suspicion.

As usual, although she looked so militant, Tara was beautifully groomed. She was wearing a pair of denim overalls, with a white voile blouse, and the rich abundance of her dark hair was perfectly styled—perhaps she has a live-in hairdresser, Nicola thought, then was struck dumb for a moment as, out of the corner of her eye, she caught Ralph's widening blue gaze resting on Tara.

No, no, don't do it, Nicola, she cautioned herself. But she did it all the same.

'Tara, I'm sorry—uh—may I introduce you, and would you like to join us? Ralph, this is Tara Wells,' she said, without waiting for a reply, and right on cue Ralph stood up and smiled his shy, dazzling smile at Tara.

That was how Nicola came to drive back to Yorkeys Knob on her own, some time later, alternating between bouts of sheer laughter and panicky fright. She'd left Ralph and Tara together at Palm Cove.

Are some men born to be toy boys? she asked herself. I mean, he seemed so genuine. On the other hand, that was a little quick to be transferring his worshipping, but I suppose I gave him good cause to be on the rebound. And didn't Tara lap it up! Oh dear, what have I done?

And such, suddenly, was her overwhelming concern, that instead of driving up the Knob she turned left at the base of the hill and took the road that wound round it towards Half Moon Bay. The Yorkeys Knob Boating Club and Half Moon Bay Marina were at the end of it. There was also a boat ramp and, beside its rock walls, a little crescent of beach directly below the Knob.

She parked her car in the marina car park and walked across to the beach. There was only a young mother with a little boy of about two on the beach, and he was investigating all the rock pools.

Nicola sat down on the sand, hugged her knees and stared seaward—although her thoughts were drawn irresistibly upwards. She couldn't see the house, but if you could have scaled the cliff face of the Knob, it wasn't that far away. At least, she reflected, with the children around, Brett and Marietta would have to be civilised.

But the thing that she hadn't had time to examine in any detail was the way Brett had kissed her. Hungrily, passionately—and differently, she mused. Not like the other night, when I got the feeling he was always standing just a little outside of things, controlling them. She grimaced, and felt herself colour, but forced herself to think on. So, why the difference?

Because it would be much simpler to stay married to me. The thought slid into her mind. So, might he have been…trying to offer me more than a whole lot of plusses like a checklist? But why simpler for him?

The answer came with the memory of the client he'd gone to see in the watch-house that morning and what he himself had said—'Who knows *what* we're really like under the surface?' Did that mean that the intensity of what he still felt for Marietta could also be dangerous? And that was why it was not only simpler but safer to be married to Nicola, who was ideal on every other score but did not arouse that dangerous degree of passion in him?

She came out of her reverie with a sigh, and with the conviction that she might just have hit the nail on the head. Then she rose slowly, brushed the sand off and decided she had to go home. Only to discover, when she got back to her car, that the curious angle it had acquired was due to a very flat tyre.

'Where *have* you been—and where's Ralph?' Marietta demanded.

It was dark by now, past seven o'clock, and Nicola was filthy and exhausted. With the aid of a couple of brawny yachting types from the marina her tyre had been changed, but the spare had barely got her out of the car park before subsiding, with a rush of air, to the rim.

Her helpers had been delighted to be of even more assistance, and they'd organised a vehicle to convey her and the tyre to the local garage, which had been almost back on the highway, where it had been deemed unrepairable. So she'd had to buy a new one, and then be conveyed back to have it fitted to the car.

She glanced at Marietta and Brett. They were seated at the dining room table and there was no sign of the children, but the sound of television was coming from the den. And there were the remains of what looked like a dish of spaghetti bolognese on the table, with a salad and a half-finished bottle of Chianti.

Marietta had discarded her boots and pulled the velvet ribbon out of her hair, but for once she looked tense and irritable, and a swift glance at Brett revealed a hard, cold line to his mouth.

'I had a puncture,' Nicola said laconically

'Where? And why the hell didn't you call me?' Brett said angrily.

Nicola stiffened. 'At the marina, as a matter of fact, and I had plenty of help, thank you.'

'What on earth where you doing at the marina?' he queried, his eyes grim. 'Planning to *sail* to Tibet?'

Nicola drew a deep breath, but before she could speak Marietta intervened. 'None of this explains what you've done with Ralph,' she pointed out satirically.

Nicola cut her extremely confrontational exchange of glances with her husband and switched to his first wife. 'I'll tell you what I've done with him, Marietta, but before I do so you should be ashamed of yourself. Not only is he an archetypal toy boy, but he's an awfully long way from home. However, he's transferred his somewhat transitory affections to Tara Wells.'

Marietta knocked over her wine glass and Brett

stood up. 'What the devil are you talking about, Nicola?' he said harshly.

'Did you still want Tara for yourself, Brett?' Nicola smiled ingenuously. 'Sorry, but I imagine she might be pretty taken up with Ralph for a while.'

Brett swore, then strode over to her. 'Enough of this,' he said through his teeth. 'Just tell me in words of one syllable what happened.'

'No problem, Brett,' Nicola replied, but her eyes were a deep, furious blue. 'I took Ralph to lunch at Palm Cove. While we were discussing the ludicrous state of affairs in this household, not to mention his unfortunate penchant for falling for older women, who should tap me on the shoulder but Tara? For some reason she seems to haunt me,' she said with scathing irony.

'So,' she went on, 'I introduced them, and before you could say Jiminy Cricket Ralph had got over his trauma at the thought of how you were using him, Marietta, and Tara—well, Tara was just *lapping* him up,' she finished with supreme mockery.

Marietta put her hands to her face. Nicola closed her eyes and prayed again as Marietta made a choking sound—that turned out to be laughter. 'Nicky,' she said unsteadily, 'you didn't.'

'I did,' Nicola confirmed, and turned back to Brett. 'Someone had to do something. But there's more. I think I've served my purpose well and truly now, so I'll be going on to better things, Brett—and don't expect me to be here for my birthday. Oh, one last word of wisdom for the two of you. Just think of how much your children love you.'

He reached for her, but she stepped backwards, and

the expression in her eyes was stern, proud and withering. He dropped his hand to his side and she walked away, once again to the seclusion of her bedroom. But this time she locked herself in. And this time she started to pack.

CHAPTER EIGHT

AT MIDNIGHT, Nicola looked around at the colourful chaos of her room. Her unicorn poster had been unhooked from the wall and she'd packed as many of her clothes as she had suitcase space for—less than half of them. She'd also turned on her bedside radio, so that she would be unable to hear anything that was transpiring beyond the four walls of her room.

It's a start, she told herself tiredly. I could never take everything in one go anyway. There are books, music, all the odds and ends one acquires in two years—not to mention the odds and ends one came with in the first place.

Then her gaze fell on the plans Richard had brought over two nights ago, and the contract, and she sat down on the bed with a sigh.

Just as well I didn't get around to signing it, she mused, with her chin in her hands. Apart from the problems of finding a workshop and a kiln, I won't be in Cairns for a while. Where will I be, though?

Tibet? Africa? Strange how they seem to have lost their gloss—not that I was enamoured of Tibet in the first place. Europe, then, and the UK? My mother's family came from…somewhere over there.

She lay back suddenly, then curled up into a ball and drifted off to sleep.

When she woke the next morning, she found that someone had cleared the bed, turned her radio off and

covered her up with a quilt from the spare bedroom.
It was a moment before she remembered that she'd
locked her doors.

She sat up abruptly. The bedroom doors locked on
the inside by means of pressing in a button on the
handle; they could be unlocked on the outside by a
master key—a safeguard against the children locking
themselves into their rooms. So far as she knew, she
had one on her keyring and so did Brett. Had he…?

Then she saw that her unicorn poster was back up
on the wall—she'd had to stand on a chair to unhook
it, and Marietta wouldn't be tall enough to hook it up
again without a chair. Surely she wouldn't have slept
through that—and, anyway, why would Marietta
bother?

Brett, she thought, and rubbed her face. Is he still
determined not to let me go? What do I have to do
to make him *see*…?

But after a shower, and dressing, she discovered
that only Ellen and the children were home.

'It is Monday,' Ellen said reasonably, after Nicola
had asked her where everyone was. She was setting
out breakfast for Chris and Sasha, both waiting ex-
pectantly at the table in the family room.

'I know, but it's also quite early,' Nicola objected
a bit lamely, and kissed the children good morning.

'Well, don't forget he had the day off on Friday,
and anyway, he said to tell you he has an early court
appearance this morning—said you'd know what it
was about.'

'Oh, yes,' Nicola murmured. 'What about
Marietta?' she mouthed to Ellen, over Chris and
Sasha's heads.

'Haven't the foggiest,' Ellen said cheerfully.

'Mummy's gone to Sydney to see about her new job,' Sasha said importantly, causing Nicola and Ellen to exchange rueful glances. 'And Daddy said I could have one more day off school to help you with Chris, because Ellen is only working half a day today, aren't you?'

'Feel a bit guilty about that, but I've got a dentist appointment,' Ellen said ruefully. 'Got this nagging toothache that's beginning to drive me mad. Brett said he was sure you could cope, though. Said he wouldn't be late home.'

'He…oh, of course,' Nicola agreed, although what she felt like screaming was, *And what else did he have to say? Anything about this being absolute blackmail?*

Then, midway through the afternoon, Brett's secretary Margaret rang with the news that Brett had been unexpectedly called to Brisbane.

'Brisbane!' Nicola said incredulously. 'What on earth for?'

Margaret explained in great detail. A large corporation that they acted for was suing a competitor over what they considered to be unfair trade practices. The case, set down for hearing in the Supreme Court in Brisbane, had been due to start today but their representative had taken ill—on the floor of the court, would you believe!—and Brett had flown down to step into his shoes.

'How long is he likely to be away?' Nicola asked faintly.

'It could be a while, Mrs Harcourt,' Margaret said cautiously. 'Although there's always the hope that they'll settle out of court. But it came up so unexpectedly, he really didn't have time to turn around. He did ask me to tell you to get Ellen to come and sleep in with you. He was most particular that that should be done—on account of poor young Christian and his broken leg. And if there's anything I can do…?'

'No. Thank you, Margaret.' Nicola put the phone down and rubbed her face, her mind in chaos. Surely he could have sent somebody else? Why not Tara— unless she'd gone AWOL with Ralph? And why hadn't he rung her himself? Why would he leave Chris at this time? Not that she couldn't cope, but…

'He's got such a lot on his plate,' Ellen said with a click of her tongue when she got back from the dentist. 'Not to worry. I'll just ring my sister and tell her to water my plants!'

'Look—I can do it,' Chris said excitedly, and hopped across the floor on his crutches.

'Your dad will be real proud of you when he gets home,' Ellen said.

'Where's he gone?' Sasha asked.

Nicola forced herself to concentrate. 'He's had to go down to Brisbane for a big trial in the Supreme Court. It's very important.'

'Will he have to wear a wig and a red coat?' Chris asked.

'No, that's the judge, silly,' Sasha said. 'I 'spect he'll be assisting the barrier.'

'The barrister—you are a clever girl, Sash,' Nicola said admiringly.

Sasha swelled with pride, then said immediately, 'But you're not going anywhere, are you, Nicola?'

'No, darling,' Nicola heard herself say gaily. 'You know me.'

He rang that night, before the children were asleep. Nicola was the last to speak to him as Ellen shooed Sasha and Chris off to bed.

'Sorry about this,' he said.

'No more than I,' she answered stiffly. 'It doesn't change how I feel.'

'But you'll stay?' His voice was clipped and weary-sounding, and she was enough of a lawyer's daughter and wife to know that taking over a brief at this stage of the proceedings was a mammoth task.

She sighed. 'Brett, I have no choice but to stay. You know that.'

'Why don't you start on your clam fountain?'

She frowned. 'I'm not sure I'll be doing it now.'

'Do it, Nicola,' he said tiredly. 'Whatever happens between us, it can only benefit you. Look—' she heard a bell ring in the background '—I have to go now, but I'll ring every evening about this time. Goodnight.' And he put the phone down.

Nicola took the receiver from her ear and stared at it bemusedly.

But the next morning she did as he'd said, although she rang Richard and explained how Brett still hadn't had time to go over the contract and that she didn't like to sign it until he did.

'But you'll make a start?'

'I…yes.' She moved uneasily, because she wasn't being essentially truthful—the truth being that she *would* make a start, if only to give herself something to do in case she went round the bend, but she had no idea if she would ever be able to finish it.

'Can I come round?' Richard asked as the silence lengthened.

'No. I—not while he's not here, Richard.'

'Have you had a chance to think over what I said?'

She flinched, because she hadn't but didn't want to hurt him. 'I'm very honoured,' she said quietly. 'But—'

'You're in love with him, aren't you, Nicola? Whatever has happened in your marriage hasn't changed that, has it?'

'No—and yes, I am, Richard. If I ever gave you cause to think otherwise, I'm truly sorry.'

'You didn't—except when you asked me whether I had a wife tucked away down south.'

'That's what I mean.' She swallowed.

'I wondered if you were thinking of using me to make him jealous?'

This is a nightmare, Nicola thought, and could think of not a thing to say.

'I can wait,' he said then, somewhat wryly. 'You never know—and I'd hate to lose my clam fountain in the meantime. When he gets back I'll be in touch.' The line went dead.

People seem to be making a habit of hanging up on me, she thought dryly, then frowned as another thought hit her. Surely Marietta could have postponed *her* departure? She'd been so genuinely anguished not to have been around for Chris, but now this? It didn't make sense. Unless—had whatever passed between her and Brett been so catastrophic she'd just…run?

In the event of not being able to understand *any-*

thing, she took Chris down to the shed in the garden with her—Sasha had gone to school reluctantly—and they spent the morning there. Both the children had always been fascinated by her pottery, and she gave Chris some clay to play with. It kept him happy for hours while she got down to work of a more serious nature.

In fact, over the next few days her clam fountain proved to be a godsend. It kept her mind off the worst of her problems and gave the children something to occupy them as they got right into the spirit of it, with drawings, suggestions and their own little clay models.

Brett rang each night, as promised, but she kept their conversations to the basics. Marietta also rang several times, but, whether by design or sheer coincidence, Nicola was either out shopping or in the shower or in the shed for all of these calls.

Then she woke up one morning and realised her twenty-first birthday was only a day away. How bizarre, she thought. He must have forgotten. They've all forgotten. No party, no key of the door, no nothing. Why had he been so insistent about it if he could forget it so easily?

That evening, long after the children were asleep and Ellen had gone to bed too, she was reading in the lounge with her feet curled under her. There was a lamp on, on the table beside the settee, but the rest of the lounge-dining area was dim and shadowy.

She'd changed into a loose, silky, full-length robe, navy blue with pink and white birds of paradise on it, and soon she put her book down with a sigh and contemplated the irony that she, who had been rather scathing about twenty-first birthdays, had never felt lonelier and more let down in her life.

She laid her head back and closed her eyes. She knew what would happen, but couldn't prevent it. The wings of her mind took her to Brett, in a hotel room, in Brisbane, probably seated at a desk or a table littered with papers, with his tie pulled loose and his shirtsleeves pushed up and that razor-sharp mind preparing tomorrow's agenda for the case.

Tired? Possibly. But he had the ability to push himself to the limit, she well knew. Her father had often commented on it. Lonely? Who knew? But, if so, who he was lonely for was another mystery. Marietta? Tara? Me—no, not me, she corrected herself. And I don't really believe Tara was a serious thing with him now, so...

Her lashes lifted at a sound, and she sat up suddenly with her heart in her mouth—because there was the outline of a tall figure beyond the circle of lamplight, although she'd heard nothing else in her preoccupation.

'Brett?' she said, blinking furiously. 'Is it you or am I dreaming—?' She broke off abruptly.

'Yes. Dreaming?' he said, and moved forward so she could see him clearly.

He wore a grey suit, white shirt and a charcoal tie with gold stripes, and he had a briefcase which he dropped to the floor.

'I...I didn't hear the car, or the door, and I certainly wasn't expecting you,' she said. 'So that's why I thought I was dreaming.' She stopped again, and clasped her hands together.

'You didn't think I'd forgotten your birthday, Nicola?' he said dryly, and sat down opposite her.

She licked her lips, and to gain time and composure studied him. Although he looked well-groomed enough to take his place in a courtroom, there were lines of weariness beside his mouth—and she said the first thing that came to mind. 'That's a new tie and suit. At least, I don't think I've ever seen them before.'

His lips twisted. 'I left in such a rush, I had to kit myself out in Brisbane.'

'Of course. So it's over—have they settled out of court or something?' she asked, wide-eyed.

'No. If anything, they've dug in for a long and bitter battle.'

'I don't understand,' she whispered.

'I've replaced myself. With Tara.' He grimaced.

'I wondered why you didn't do that in the first place,' Nicola said honestly. 'Not that I know the finer points of it, or that it's any of my business—'

'As a matter of fact, it is.'

Nicola stared at him. He had his arms stretched along the armrests, his legs sprawled out in front of him, and he was beating a little tattoo with the fingers of one hand on the oatmeal linen. He was watching his fingers, with his head inclined downwards and sideways, and once again the lamplight was picking out the chestnut in his brown hair.

'In what way?' she asked uncertainly.

He said nothing for a moment, then looked up with something in his hazel eyes that she couldn't decipher, except to wonder whether she was imagining that it was sheer, self-directed mockery. 'It was the only way

I could devise to…keep my hands off you until your twenty-first birthday, Nicola.'

Her lips parted incredulously and her heart started to beat heavily. 'Why?'

'*Why?*' A glint of irony lit his eyes and a nerve beat in his jaw. 'Because none of the strategies I've employed over the last two years were the least help once I'd—kissed you. You may remember what happened two days after Marietta got home?'

'But…' Her voice failed her.

'Still don't understand, Nicola? Then I'll explain. Shades of Richard Holloway,' he said grimly, 'but I realised I was in love with you the night I asked you to marry me.'

She gasped. 'That can't be true!'

'Oh, it's true,' he murmured.

'But what…but *why*…?' Her eyes were huge and dark with incomprehension.

He laid his head back tiredly. 'I made a promise to your father when he was dying that I would do my level best to stop you from marrying until you were at least twenty-one. I broke the letter of that promise, but I knew I could never break the spirit of it. Not only on his behalf but on my own—and especially on yours.'

Nicola was transfixed. 'He…did *that*? He didn't tell me.'

'Naturally not,' Brett said quietly.

She bit her lip. 'You could have told me.'

He only looked at her.

She stood up shakily. 'Brett, if this is true, do you mean to tell me you've…put me through two years of a marriage of convenience just because of a—a *date*?'

Something flickered in his eyes. But he said evenly, 'Not just a date, Nicola. The defining of a period for you to settle after the trauma of his death, to find your feet without being burdened down with loneliness—loneliness that might have caused you to seek solace unwisely.'

'To grow up—you missed that one,' she said hoarsely.

He shrugged wearily. 'Nineteen is not so grown up.'

'But...but once it happened, once you did kiss me...' she stammered. 'I was almost twenty-one anyway.'

'And Richard Holloway was on the horizon,' he pointed out significantly. 'You were also showing distinct signs of wanting to spread your wings, and that kiss—'

'I know. I started it,' she said hollowly. 'But, well, I *did* start it.' She gazed at him, willing him to understand why.

He smiled, but with not much amusement. 'Prompted by Tara.'

She sat down again slowly. 'Let me get this straight. For two years you never gave me one sign of how you felt so you could keep a promise to my father—Brett, that's...that's... How did you *do* it?'

'As a matter of fact, it took more self-control than I thought I was capable of, but there are ways. You just don't allow yourself to dwell on it. You work like the devil and—' he shrugged '—I've had other less than easy periods in my life. This was one more.'

Nicola was silent, and she was suddenly assailed by the memory that Brett had four younger brothers and sisters, now scattered around the country, all successful, all having fulfilled their mother's wish before she had died—that they get university degrees—and all given an enormous amount of support by Brett. She remembered what a bitter blow it had been to Brett that their mother shouldn't have been able to live to see all their success.

A man of steel, she thought, toughened and hardened by adversity, and a man who honoured his promises—yes, perhaps it was possible that he'd endured two years of living in the same house with her and loving her, but...

She frowned as an element of doubt plagued her, and something else pricked her consciousness before finding expression—this didn't have the authentic ring of a happy outcome.

'Well...' She hesitated. 'That may be, but now you're going to tell me you're going back to Marietta, aren't you? For Chris and Sasha's sake? Are you trying to let me down lightly, Brett?'

He sat up abruptly. 'No. Nicola—'

'But she wants it. You told me so yourself. And don't think I couldn't work it out, with some help from Ellen—' She stopped, and could have bitten her tongue.

He said incredulously, 'Help from *Ellen*?'

Nicola sighed. 'She...it was the only time she ever discussed it with me. Normally she's the soul of discretion—'

'So why did she change—and when was this?'

'Just before Marietta got home—when Chris broke

his leg. She—' Nicola moved uncomfortably '—she's never forgiven Marietta for deserting them, and she was...annoyed enough about her coming home to "steal the limelight", as she put it, to dredge up a conversation between you that she'd overheard—or more like a row.' She shrugged.

'Which one was that?' he asked wearily.

Nicola stared at him. 'Over whose career was the more important, when she said...if you'd only give her five years, she'd be anything you wanted her to be,' she said bleakly.

'That was—'

'Brett, no.' Nicola sat forward intently. 'Don't you see how it all fits in? It *suited* her to have you married to me. It took care of the kids, took care of *me*—and it kept you out of other women's clutches. Why do you think she took such an instantaneous dislike to Tara? Tell me I'm wrong, Brett.'

'You're not wrong. But that was never *my* plan, Nicola.'

'What about her plans?' she whispered. 'You just said I wasn't wrong. And Ellen thought that Marietta never believed you would do it—divorce her. On top of that, I'm quite *sure* she only brought Ralph home to make you jealous. She wouldn't let him sleep with her.'

He raised a wry eyebrow and was silent for a moment. Then he said, 'Perhaps. And for what it's worth, Nicola, she was spurred on by you yourself. She couldn't believe you could be so complacent about Tara, for one thing—'

'Complacent!' Nicola echoed incredulously.

'She did only see you together once—that night—

the only time she saw Tara, for that matter, but she marvelled at how composed you were. And for another thing you seemed so determined to throw us together and get rid of the toy boy. She knows you well, and she said to me, "You haven't done it, have you, Brett? I'll bet she's still as pure as she was the day you married her."'

Nicola swallowed.

'But the thing was, she'd completely miscalculated the reason *why* I hadn't done it. Nicola, I told you once how it happened between Marietta and me—'

'You told me so I'd not make a fuss about Tara— oh, hell!' She rubbed her face agitatedly. 'But what was I supposed to think? You'd never talked about it before. Then this strange woman waltzed in and virtually took over! I know you've always denied it, but how could you not have known Tara was—smitten?' she said bitterly.

'Tara never had anything to do with—anything. All right, yes, I knew,' he said, and grimaced. 'I couldn't help wondering whether it would make you jealous.

'But,' he went on, when she could only open her mouth soundlessly, 'the only reason I told you the absolute truth about how whatever it was I'd felt for Marietta had literally burnt itself out was because this day was approaching, and I needed you to understand what you'd never understood before.'

Nicola licked her lips and swallowed. 'So...?'

'So you would be able to believe me when I told you why I asked you to marry me.' He paused, then went on, 'I can remember it so clearly—the dress you were wearing, with little pearl buttons down the front, how blue your eyes were, how clean and shining your hair was, how unhappy you were. And I knew in a flash that I wanted you, needed you and loved you—because you were not only unique to me but simply unique. It was as if you were a part of me, but not a child any longer. I wanted you,' he said barely audibly, 'in the most desperate way a man can want a woman.'

'Brett,' she whispered.

'Wait,' he said gently. 'So I did the only thing I could without breaking the spirit of my promise to your father—and that was bad enough. And, although you may never know how much it cost, I tried to give you a happy, comfortable life, untouched by any of the—darker, deeper side of things that you seemed not to be remotely interested in anyway.'

'Until I grew up,' she said, and felt a tear drop onto her hand.

'Yes. Then, just when I thought I was getting into the home straight—just when I was beginning to wonder whether underneath that exterior which was always determined to give me as good as you got—' his lips twisted '—there might be more—you suddenly became determined to leave me.'

'I—'

'Let me finish, Nicola. I began to think that what I might have done was smother you with the children and actually slow down the process rather than the opposite. Was I right?'

'Do you mean…?'

'I mean, on top of the sudden desire to leave and the general discontent, there was Richard Holloway.'

Her throat worked, then she slipped off the chair suddenly and came to sit at his feet. 'Richard

Holloway,' she said, 'was the Reverend Callam's invention, not mine. And Richard knows now what happened.'

Brett frowned down at her. 'The marriage counsellor—with the un-Christian notions?'

'Yes. You see, when I went to see him—the Reverend, that is—he was...he couldn't agree that I should give up on this marriage without one last...test. He said there was a tried and tested way of getting a man to reveal himself in these matters and that was to make him jealous. Poor Richard simply happened to be on the spot when I still had that advice on my mind.'

'Make me jealous? Is that what he suggested?' he said slowly. 'Why would he suggest that?'

Nicola smiled at him through her tears. 'I told him the only reason I'd agreed to this marriage of convenience in the first place was because I was in love with you and I'd hoped to be able to take Marietta's place in your heart. But that I'd had almost two years to find out that it was never going to happen and I couldn't...live with it any longer.'

'Nicola, you may have thought that,' he said with an effort, 'but the last time I kissed you it was a different matter, wasn't it?'

'No—you must have a short memory, Brett.'

'On the contrary, I have the clearest recollection of how you looked—horrified.'

'That was...that was after I realised Marietta and the children had arrived, Brett, and I thought you were using me for several reasons.'

'What reasons?' he said, on a suddenly indrawn breath.

'To prove to Marietta you'd got over her—because what was between the two of you was much too dangerous. Much simpler to be married to me, because I fitted the bill in every way and would never provoke those dangerous emotions in you.'

'*Dangerous?*'

'Brett, don't you remember? That very morning you'd been to see someone in the watch-house who had almost shot his wife.'

'Oh that. Yes, I remember, but—'

'You said—"Who knows *what* we're really like under the surface?" I thought you meant that underneath you could be in trouble with what you felt for Marietta—especially since she'd taken to parading a toy boy in front of you.'

'I…' Some the lines eased beside his mouth and he took her hand. 'I *was* in trouble, Nicola, but only because I was very tempted to…pick you up and run off with you. Away from Marietta and her machinations and her toy boys, and even from her children.'

Nicola gasped. 'Your children, too.'

'I know, I know. It was only a momentary impulse. But when you looked like that…' He stopped and sighed. 'I was confronted by another problem. I was going to have to let you go.'

'Brett—' her hand moved in his '—if I can believe what you've told me, can you believe what I told the Reverend Callam?'

A faint smile lit his eyes. 'I'm beginning to have nightmares about the Reverend Callam.' The smile died. 'What did you tell him, Nicola?'

'That while I may have been in love with you I wasn't so young and immature as to let you see it, and that what it really amounted to was my pride wouldn't let me show you.'

'He—believed you?'

'*He* believed me. Are *you* going to? Because if you're trying to tell me I need longer to grow up, or something like that, I'll die a little, I think. Two years is a very long time to be pretending... Oh, thank God,' she whispered as he suddenly swept her up into his arms.

'Happy birthday,' he said softly, later—quite some time later.

'Have I really made it?'

She was lying in his arms; they were lying together on the settee. Her robe was open and his hands were beneath it. He'd kissed her until she could no longer have a single doubt that this was a man who'd wanted her for two long years.

'I asked you how you did it,' she murmured, and traced the line of his jaw.

'Kept my hands off you?'

'Mmm...but I had the same problem,' she confided. 'So, whilst Tara may have given me the impetus to do it, it was only what I'd been secretly dying to do for so long.'

'Kiss me?'

'Yes, Brett,' she said demurely, although her eyes sparkled with laughter. But she sobered abruptly. 'Then I felt terrible.'

'You didn't know what *I* was going through,' he commented. 'Can I tell you what one of my worst moments was?'

She pillowed her head on her arms and he played

with her locket, then his fingers slipped downwards. 'Yes,' she said, but with a tremor.

'That night on the beach. I was seriously tempted to forget any promises I'd ever made because there was something about you in the firelight that was...' He stopped, then held her hard.

'You must—you *were* a mind-reader. Because I'd had this extraordinary fantasy, about a tent and just the two of us on a wild beach with wild animals...' She trailed off ruefully as he lifted his head and looked into her eyes quizzically. 'Well, you were the one who taught me about fantasies.'

'There was another time that was an extreme test of my self-control.'

'There was?'

'Yes,' he agreed gravely. 'After that school presentation. When you were so annoyed, then so sweet and so amused to think how you'd surprised me. And you walked away from me down the drive, swinging your hat—I very nearly made this a very proper marriage in every sense of the word there and then. And that was before I kissed you for the first time, my darling Nicola—but this is no fantasy, is it?' he said, suddenly sober.

She took her hands from behind her head and slid them round his neck. 'No. Because I can't wait to be taught how to make love to you, Brett. And if you ever have any doubts, will you think of this? The only reason I wanted to give you back to Marietta was because I loved you too much to think of you living with second best—and because of Chris and Sasha.'

'Sweetheart,' he said with an effort, then lifted her to a sitting position.

Her eyes widened.

'Don't look like that. There are just one or two formalities I'd like to deal with before—well, can you be patient for a moment?'

'I...yes,' she said.

He kissed her lips lightly and closed her robe. Then he got up and walked away. But he wasn't gone long. He came back with a bottle of champagne and two glasses. He said, as he removed the gold foil and popped the cork, 'I was going to wait for this, but I think we could do with it. Have a sip.'

She took the foaming glass and did as she was bid.

'First of all—' he sat down beside her and put his arm round her shoulders '—Marietta knows everything now. And in typical Marietta fashion she has made the necessary adjustments. You see...'

He paused and studied his glass. 'Circumstance, and guilt about Sasha and Chris, made it look like a good idea for her to come back. But when I forced her to admit to herself that without those two things her career would still have taken precedence over us, she realised what I'd known for years—that the flame had gone out.'

Nicola took another sip, and blinked and sniffed.

'And she sent you a message,' he went on. 'She said to tell you—and by the way, she connived at you being here alone with the kids, so you couldn't run away from me.'

'She did? I wondered about that!'

He smiled, and kissed the top of her head. 'She said to tell you that she'd never felt more ashamed in her life than after what you said, and that now you wouldn't have to worry about Chris and Sasha being with her, which they will be on a fairly regular basis. She also said—''Be happy, Nicky darling, with my sincerest blessings—I wish that for you more than anything else in the world. Not only because I love you, but because of what you've done for the kids.'''

Nicola burst into tears. He took her glass and held her close until the storm subsided, then dried her tears with his handkerchief.

'Sorry,' she said huskily. 'But...but that's Marietta for you.'

'That's Marietta for you,' he agreed. 'Have we finally laid to rest that—spectre?'

'Yes. *Yes*. I mean, if you wouldn't go back for the sake of Sasha and Chris...'

'Exactly, but not only that. Most importantly because of you.'

'I...' She paused, then formed the words she'd never said. 'I love you, Brett.'

'Thank God,' he murmured, and drew something out of his pocket.

'What's that?'

'I was going to give it to you before we got married, but you objected rather strenuously.' He clicked open a rather battered little leather box. There was a sapphire engagement ring in it. 'It was my mother's,' he said quietly. 'But you could have one of your very own if you'd like.'

She drew a trembling breath. 'No. Oh, Brett, thank you so much. I'll...I will always treasure it.'

He took it out of the box and slid it on in front of her wedding band. It fitted perfectly. He looked from it into her shining eyes and said, 'There is one more convention we did away with at the time.'

'What was that?'

'A honeymoon. And before you worry about the kids—'

'No,' she said. 'I mean, no, I won't. And I can't think of anything I'd rather do than be alone with you.'

'Good. Not that we can go tomorrow—'

'Why not?'

He laughed and kissed her. 'It's—well, it might take at least a day to organise.'

'Then might I be allowed to show you what I've been bottling up inside me for longer than two years?' she asked gravely. 'Seeing that I'm not only twenty-one now, but your wife?'

He smiled down at her with his heart in his eyes.

'I would be both proud and honoured, Mrs Harcourt.'

'How often have I longed to do this?' he said very quietly.

Her bedroom was almost in darkness, with only one bedside lamp on. Their clothes were scattered on the floor and they were lying on the bed. Brett had his head propped on his hand and he was just staring at her naked body, as if drinking it in. Then he raised his other hand and drew it down the curve of her hip.

She trembled finely, and touched her palm to his cheek. 'You may never know—you said that to me—how much I've longed for it too. Perhaps...' she smiled faintly, a wise little smile '...I was a little more grown up than you ever knew?'

He traced the swell of one breast, then the other, and bent his head to taste her nipples.

She arched her body against him and wrapped her arms around his shoulders, revelling in the glorious contact with the whole lean, strong length of him.

'Perhaps,' he said softly. 'But you do understand why I held back, don't you? I—'

'Of course—your integrity is another reason why I love you so much,' she murmured, and kissed his throat.

'Then I have to tell you I can't stand much more of this, my darling,' he said into her hair.

'Don't,' she whispered. 'The freedom of my body is yours, Brett.'

He said her name on a suddenly tortured breath, and started to kiss her.

There was a surprise for her that morning, Saturday.

She got up very late—later than Brett—to find that the house had been transformed into a wonderland of white ribbons and silver balloons. To find Sasha and Chris dressed in their best clothes and about to expire from serious over-excitement. To find a champagne luncheon for at least twenty people laid out in the dining room and a magnificent cake with twenty-one candles.

'But...but I thought you'd all forgotten,' she stammered.

'Nearly bust a gut getting them to keep the secret,' Ellen said, and inclined her head towards Sasha and Chris.

'I told you we wouldn't tell, Ellen,' Sasha reproved, and added to Nicola, 'Daddy had it all under control—even when he had to be in Brisbane.'

Nicola turned to Brett. He held out his hand and

she took it, managing to say huskily, 'Thank you. I...thank you. I guess I'd better get changed.' She looked ruefully down at her shorts and T-shirt.

'May I make a suggestion?' he murmured. 'Why don't you wear your wedding dress?'

So she did—although she didn't wear the hat—and it turned out to be a lively party, with their best friends, Ellen's family and the special delivery of a magnificent basket of flowers—from Marietta.

Nicola was still in her beautiful dress as the sun started to set and the last guests left. She and Brett were standing on the deck, hand in hand, watching the changing colours of the sea.

'Happy?' he asked.

'More than you could believe.'

'About last night...' he murmured.

Nicola caught her breath and remembered their lovemaking—not that it had been far from her mind all day.

'I was wondering whether it lived up to expectations, that's all.' He looked down at her gravely.

She stared into his hazel eyes and recalled being possessed by him with a need and a hunger that had surpassed all her expectations. But it had also touched a response in her so profound it had carried them both into territory where she would never again feel less than equal with this tall man. Never again not know that she was both his haven and his match.

And when they'd come down from the star-shot splendour that had racked them simultaneously, and he'd cradled her in his arms and smoothed her damp hair from her brow, smudged the tears of joy from her cheeks, she'd offered up a little prayer of thanks for the impulse that had taken her to see the Reverend Peter Callam those short weeks ago.

'About last night...' she said, equally as grave. 'I can think of only one word to describe it.'

'And that is?' He raised an eyebrow.

'Well, two. Absolutely awesome.'

'My own thinking entirely, as it happens. It also happens that I haven't given you your twenty-first birthday present yet.'

'But I thought...?' She glanced down at the sapphire ring on her finger.

'No. That signifies something else, Nicola. This is—this is something I had specially made for you. At the time, I didn't know whether I'd be able to tell you this, but...' He paused, and put something into her hand.

She looked down to see a tiny gold key, studded with diamonds, on a fine chain.

'Tell me what, Brett?' Her voice shook because of what she saw in his eyes.

'That without you to hold this key, the key of my heart, I'm lost and alone—darling, don't cry.'

'I'm not,' she said tremulously. 'Yes, I am. Oh, Brett!' She went into his arms and he held her agonisingly close.

'Were you ever wrong, Sash!' Chris said in a stage-whisper as they peeped out of the lounge windows.

'Well, I can't be right all the time,' Sasha replied reasonably. 'Do you think they're going to do this all the time now they've started?' she added with a frown.

'You were the one who gave them the idea!'

'Come away, you two!' Ellen commanded gruffly.

Brett and Nicola broke apart, then looked at each other and began to laugh helplessly.

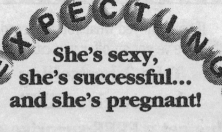

If you enjoyed what you just read,
then we've got an offer you can't resist!

Take 2 bestselling
love stories FREE!

Plus get a FREE surprise gift!

Clip this page and mail it to Harlequin Reader Service®

IN U.S.A.	IN CANADA
3010 Walden Ave.	P.O. Box 609
P.O. Box 1867	Fort Erie, Ontario
Buffalo, N.Y. 14240-1867	L2A 5X3

YES! Please send me 2 free Harlequin Presents® novels and my free surprise gift. Then send me 6 brand-new novels every month, which I will receive months before they're available in stores. In the U.S.A., bill me at the bargain price of $3.12 plus 25¢ delivery per book and applicable sales tax, if any*. In Canada, bill me at the bargain price of $3.49 plus 25¢ delivery per book and applicable taxes**. That's the complete price and a savings of over 10% off the cover prices—what a great deal! I understand that accepting the 2 free books and gift places me under no obligation ever to buy any books. I can always return a shipment and cancel at any time. Even if I never buy another book from Harlequin, the 2 free books and gift are mine to keep forever. So why not take us up on our invitation. You'll be glad you did!

106 HEN CNER
306 HEN CNES

Name	(PLEASE PRINT)
Address	Apt.#
City	State/Prov.	Zip/Postal Code

* Terms and prices subject to change without notice. Sales tax applicable in N.Y.
** Canadian residents will be charged applicable provincial taxes and GST.
   All orders subject to approval. Offer limited to one per household.
   ® are registered trademarks of Harlequin Enterprises Limited.

PRES99   ©1998 Harlequin Enterprises Limited

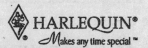

HARLEQUIN ⬥ PRESENTS®

THE BARONS

One sister, three brothers— who will inherit, and will they all find lovers?

Jonas is approaching his eighty-fifth birthday, and he's decided it's time to choose the heir of his sprawling ranch, Espada. He has three ruggedly good-looking sons, Gage, Travis and Slade, and a beautiful stepdaughter, Caitlin.

Who will receive Baron's bequest? As the Baron brothers and their sister discover, there's more at stake than Espada. For love also has its part to play in deciding their futures....

Enjoy Gage's story:
Marriage on the Edge
Harlequin Presents #2027, May 1999

And in August, get to know Travis a whole lot better in
More than a Mistress
Harlequin Presents #2045

Available wherever Harlequin books are sold.

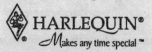

⬥ HARLEQUIN®
Makes any time special ™

Coming Next Month

HARLEQUIN PRESENTS®

THE BEST HAS JUST GOTTEN BETTER!

#2043 TO BE A HUSBAND Carole Mortimer
Bachelor Brothers
It's the first time for Jonathan that any woman has resisted his charm. What does he have to do to win over the cool, elegant Gaye Royal? Propose marriage? But being a husband is the last thing Jonathan has in mind....

#2044 THE WEDDING-NIGHT AFFAIR Miranda Lee
Society Weddings
As a top wedding coordinator, Fiona was now organizing her ex-husband's marriage. But Philip wasn't about to let their passionate past rest. Then Fiona realized that Philip's bride-to-be didn't love him...but Fiona still did!

#2045 MORE THAN A MISTRESS Sandra Marton
The Barons
When Alexandra Thorpe won the eligible Travis Baron for the weekend, she didn't claim her prize. Travis is intrigued to discover why the cool blond beauty had staked hundreds of dollars on him and then just walked away....

#2046 HOT SURRENDER Charlotte Lamb
Zoe was enraged by Connel's barefaced cheek! But he had the monopoly on sex appeal, and her feelings had become so intense that Zoe couldn't handle him in her life. But Connel always got what he wanted: her hot surrender!

#2047 THE BRIDE'S SECRET Helen Brooks
Two years ago, Marianne had left her fiancé, Hudson de Sance, in order to protect him from a blackmailer. But what would happen now Hudson had found her again, and was still determined to marry her?

#2048 THE BABY VERDICT Cathy Williams
Jessica was flattered when Bruno Carr wanted her as his new secretary. She hadn't bargained on falling for him—or finding herself pregnant with his child. Bruno had only one solution: marriage!